S0-BEA-610

"I'll go if you promise you'll divorce me. I'm not staying married to you."

A pause, then he said, "If that's what you want, but we might have to wait a few weeks."

"I'm not sleeping with you," Freja blurted.

"I don't expect you to."

As Giovanni's flat response struck like an anvil, splitting her down the middle like a chunk of redwood, she realized she had been hoping for more of a fight. Apparently, that's not what this was.

"Take your money back, too," she said distantly. "I don't need it and it's just one more headache I don't want to deal with."

"Anything else?"

Oh, he thought he could take that sardonic tone with her? She blinked fast to see him through her matted lashes.

"Take off that ring. It's a mockery that you're wearing it."

"You want to talk about mocking our marriage with what we're wearing?" His pithy tone disparaged the meringue confection piled around her. "I promised you I would put it back on and never remove it again. I won't break that vow. So no, I will not take it off." He rapped a knuckle on the window and the locks were released. "Let's go."

Canadian **Dani Collins** knew in high school that she wanted to write romance for a living. Twenty-five years later, after marrying her high school sweetheart, having two kids with him, working at several generic office jobs and submitting countless manuscripts, she got The Call. Her first Harlequin novel won the Reviewers' Choice Award for Best First in Series from *RT Book Reviews*. She now works in her own office, writing romance.

Books by Dani Collins

Harlequin Presents

Untouched Until Her Ultra-Rich Husband
Cinderella's Royal Seduction

Conveniently Wed!

Claiming His Christmas Wife

Bound to the Desert King

Sheikh's Princess of Convenience

Feuding Billionaire Brothers

A Hidden Heir to Redeem Him
Beauty and Her One-Night Baby

Innocents for Billionaires

A Virgin to Redeem the Billionaire
Innocent's Nine-Month Scandal

The Montero Baby Scandal

The Consequence He Must Claim
The Maid's Spanish Secret
Bound by Their Nine-Month Scandal

Visit the Author Profile page
at Harlequin.com for more titles.

Dani Collins

CONFESSIONS OF AN ITALIAN MARRIAGE

HARLEQUIN
PRESENTS

If you purchased this book without a cover you should be aware that this book is stolen property. It was reported as "unsold and destroyed" to the publisher, and neither the author nor the publisher has received any payment for this "stripped book."

Recycling programs
for this product may
not exist in your area.

ISBN-13: 978-1-335-89399-4

Confessions of an Italian Marriage

Copyright © 2020 by Dani Collins

All rights reserved. No part of this book may be used or reproduced in any manner whatsoever without written permission except in the case of brief quotations embodied in critical articles and reviews.

This is a work of fiction. Names, characters, places and incidents are either the product of the author's imagination or are used fictitiously. Any resemblance to actual persons, living or dead, businesses, companies, events or locales is entirely coincidental.

This edition published by arrangement with Harlequin Books S.A.

For questions and comments about the quality of this book, please contact us at CustomerService@Harlequin.com.

Harlequin Enterprises ULC
22 Adelaide St. West, 40th Floor
Toronto, Ontario M5H 4E3, Canada
www.Harlequin.com

Printed in U.S.A.

CONFESSIONS OF AN ITALIAN MARRIAGE

To the stars of Murderball who made me think "those high-octane alphas would make a great romance hero," one who patiently simmered in my head for fifteen years until bursting to life in Giovanni. And to my editor Megan, who nudges my stories in directions I hadn't considered and always makes them better.

PROLOGUE

HELL HATH NO fury like a woman whose husband faked his own death.

Freja Catalano smiled with appropriately bedazzled delight as she took a selfie in the mirrors that surrounded where she stood on the small, carpeted dais in the back of Milan's most exclusive bridal boutique.

"I can take the photo," offered the designer, Teresina. She paused in her reverent arranging of the abundant and infinitely delicate chiffon overskirt. Every inch was tastefully embroidered with white flowers and swirling vines, seed pearls and sequins. The train puddled out for six feet behind Freja's reflection.

As Freja ran her image through different filters, a tiny prickling awareness swept across her scalp and into her shoulders. She lifted her head and glanced toward the closed curtain across the archway into the front of the shop, but there was no one there, just the sound of a bridezilla complaining about a swatch of organza.

"This is fine, thanks," Freja replied absently as she tapped out her selection and started typing her caption to post online. Her stomach remained full of unsettled butterflies, though.

#FinalFitting   #BigDay   #OneMonthAway #CantWait

As Teresina pinched seams and took in the narrow band of pearl-bedecked satin that formed the waistband of the gown, she asked around pins in her mouth, "Is the photo for your mother?"

"My social feed. My mother passed when I was young." Freja added several more hashtags about bridal nerves, first love and winter weddings in New York.

"I'm so sorry. I presumed she was in Sweden and would be attending the wedding."

"No, both of my parents are gone." And the wedding that had crushed Freja's soul for them to miss had already happened. Freja had worn a simple ivory sheath and held tulips stolen from a public garden. It had been perfect.

Or so she'd believed at the time.

And since that had been a short four and a half months ago, and since her first groom had "died" three weeks later, Freja's name was dominating the click-bait headlines with variations of *Gold-Digger to Grave-Digger* troll droppings.

Not that Freja's notoriety had bothered Terasina. Freja had earned Terasina's undying loyalty by stating, "Everyone knows Milan is superior to Paris." The fact Freja had taken possession of her husband's wealth and could buy this boutique thousands of times over didn't hurt either.

Freja didn't mention she had only come here because she was confident Giovanni was in his home country.

This is what I'm spending your money on. Do you like it? She didn't write that, just finished tagging Teresina, the boutique and—

"Does your fiancé follow you?" Teresina asked with concern. "It's bad luck for him to see the dress before the wedding."

"I guess it is, isn't it?" Freja finished tagging Nels and hit Post.

Nels was a recent graduate of business law who was drowning in debt and firmly in the closet for family reasons. In exchange for stepping into Giovanni's nonexistent shoes, Freja had promised to assure Nels's terminally ill grandmother that she loved him passionately and eternally.

It was a match made in screamingly civilized practicality.

"Tell him not to peek," Teresina suggested as she straightened and gently tested the hidden banding that secured the off-the-shoulder sleeves. The bodice was made of Venetian lace exquisitely crafted to plunge in both front and back, painting Freja's torso in white flames that danced down both arms to her wrists. "I can't imagine any man seeing you like this could resist you, though."

Freja smiled weakly, not revealing that the one man she had hoped to get a rise from had very firmly resisted.

She completely ignored the agonized whisper in the back of her head that asked, *What if he's really dead?*

He wasn't. Snakes of anxiety slithered in her middle over his continued absence, but she had plenty of reasons to believe he was still alive. Okay, more like a handful of subtle coincidences and one decent piece of evidence that wasn't solid enough to prove anything, not even a robbery. When she had tried to tell

Nels she thought there was a chance her husband could be alive, however, he'd given her a look of pity and suggested she was stuck in the denial stage of grief.

Maybe she was. She had fought seeing Giovanni's true feelings toward her, right up until that final conversation.

Do you love me? Do you even want to be married?

You're behaving like a jealous shrew. Wait for me in my hotel room. I'll join you when I've finished my meeting.

He hadn't. And dead or not, Giovanni had left his fortune in her hands. She was wholly unequipped to manage it. Nels had lived on her floor when she'd been at university and had been kind enough to look over her book contract and, later, her prenuptial agreement. When she'd gone to him with the volumes of legal documents that were coming her way as a result of her husband's supposed demise, he'd been alarmed by the overreach some of Giovanni's top executives were attempting.

Freja was a millennial with pale blond hair, blue eyes, and no formal schooling until her degree in creative writing. Obviously, that meant she was a certified bubblehead who couldn't so much as recognize when a fast food outlet was trying to upsell her a super-size of fries. Her knowledge on running a multinational corporation was zero, but she was smart enough to see phrases like "irrevocable power of attorney" as the horrendous red flags that they were.

Another woman would have snatched up the reins and stared down the sexist pigs trying to take advantage of her. Freja might have, if she hadn't been brittle with grief. Meanwhile, every meeting had been full of vultures making advances, baldly trying to flatter her into a relationship as a shortcut to Giovanni's money. It was exhausting. She didn't have the stomach for it, especially not for a fortune she neither wanted nor needed.

Nels had trusted her with his secret back when she'd shyly asked him on a date because he felt so unthreatening. He had minored in corporate ethics and longed to effect change at the highest levels. Remarrying would offer her protection from the vultures, so their grand bargain had been struck.

Was it bigamy if her first husband was secretly still alive and the second marriage was only on paper? She had asked Nels, but he had given her that pitying look again and said, "I need to know you're of sound mind or we can't do this."

Giovanni was the only person who could prove it was illegal. If he wanted to burst in at the last second to stop it, fine. But she wouldn't hold her breath. She really would be the clichéd dumb blonde if she failed to get the message that her husband didn't want to be tied to her after he had *staged an explosion* to end things.

No, she accepted that their whirlwind romance had fizzled as quickly as it had flared. If that left her feeling as bleak and wraithlike as a wisp of smoke, well, she only had herself to blame. She had known there was no such thing as forever, but she'd gone ahead and fallen for him anyway. Her heart had been broken into a thousand pieces for her trouble.

"Bellissima." Teresina finished her fussing and kissed the tips of her fingers. "Shall we try it with the veil?"

The muted ping of the bell at the front silenced the squirrel-like chatter out there. It happened so abruptly, Teresina and Freja both looked toward the closed curtain. Freja's stomach clenched with apprehension.

A male voice asked to see the manager.

The hair on the back of Freja's neck stood

up. She didn't know that voice precisely, but she'd been on high alert since Giovanni's "death." The explosion had been reported as an accident, but she was convinced it had been a deliberate attempt to kill him. She understood that meant she could be a target, too.

Maybe she was paranoid. Maybe it was just a salesman. She had no reason to believe that authoritative voice was here for her. Any man who wanted to meet with her could make an appointment through her agent or Nels or any number of other channels. They wouldn't hunt her down in a wedding boutique.

But as the clerk said, "I'll see if she's available," and the silence remained absolute, a cold layer of perspiration burst onto Freja's skin.

Teresina smiled an apology and started for the curtain.

Freja forced an unbothered smile as adrenaline poured into her extremities, clenching her lungs and tightening her hand on her phone.

As Teresina slipped past the curtain, Freja moved without second-guessing her instinct. She scooped up her miles of skirt and ran silently on the toes of her five-inch heels past the door into the changing room, where she'd left her clothes and purse, past the powder room, into the administration office, where she'd first met with Teresina and seen the—

Porta di emergenza allarmata.

That's what this was. An emergency. She was alarmed.

She shoved against the lever and burst into the narrow cobblestone alley. A loud bell began to ring within the shop. The door clattered closed behind her, muffling the sound. It grew fainter as she raced toward the street, where traffic honked in its usual chaotic madness.

She was only thinking she needed witnesses. Getting arrested for stealing a dress she'd only half paid for was better than facing whatever *that* man had in store for her. She could call Nels from the police sta—

Behind her, she heard the door slam open again. Shouts sounded.

In front of her, a black SUV swerved into the sidewalk, forcing her to pull up short at the mouth of the alley. She started to pivot in hopes of squeezing past it and down the street, but the back door flung open.

"Get in," Giovanni said.

The sight of him struck like a gong, leaving her quivering. He had a shaggy black beard and dark glasses, and his black hoodie was pulled up to hide all but his familiar cheekbones, but his legs stopped above the knees and she recognized the tense line of his mouth.

Alive. Her heart soared so high, it should have shattered the sky.

At the same time, a thousand furies invaded her like a swarm of killer bees. There was no triumph in learning she was right. There was only a crippling heartbreak that he had abandoned her. If he'd been truly dead, she would have been angry, but she wouldn't have blamed him.

This, though? He had put her through horrifying hours of actually believing he was gone. She had endured his gut-wrenching funeral, convinced it was a sham. Then, two short weeks later, she'd suffered another unbearable loss that would never heal.

He'd forced her to go through all of that *alone*.

For every minute that had passed since that awful day, she had longed for him to reveal himself, but now her feet only carried her forward so she could bitterly hiss, "Go to *hell*."

"Where do you think I've been?" he growled.

"I'm calling the police!" Teresina yelled from deep in the alley. Two of Teresina's em-

ployees were recording everything on their
phones.

A man in a suit was running toward her.
She instinctively moved closer to Giovanni,
heart jamming with fear.

Giovanni's hard arm looped around her and
he dragged her into the back of the car. He
clutched the door frame for leverage, but his
strength was as annoyingly effortless as always.

She didn't fight him. In fact, once he
grabbed her out of her stasis, she helped,
kicking against the edge of the door to thrust
herself inside, desperate for whatever sanctu-
ary he offered.

They wound up in a heap on the back seat
while the man who was chasing her came up
to the open door and reached for her leg.

She screamed and kicked at him with her
sharp heels. He dodged her shoes and threw
the yards of silk in after her, then slammed
the door before he leaped into the passenger
seat in front of Giovanni.

"Go," Giovanni said to the driver, and he
pushed himself upright.

As the SUV sped into traffic, Freja rocked
deeper into the seat, stunned to her toes.

CHAPTER ONE

Six months ago...

"ARE THOSE THE MUSHROOMS?" a woman asked, catching Freja's attention as she circulated with a tray of canapés.

Freja paused at the clutch of guests perched on sectional benches in the reception hall, waiting for the ballroom doors to open. Everyone wore beaded gowns and tuxedos and one man was in a wheelchair—

"Oh, my God!"

The tray and its contents would have slipped right off her hand if he hadn't caught it with an effortless reflex.

Giovanni Catalano. She'd checked up on him through the years, so she knew him instantly. His father had been an Italian ambassador, his mother a well-known heiress. Giovanni had been left in a wheelchair by the same car crash that had killed his parents and older brother. He'd become a Paralympic athlete, then later developed software apps that had earned him obscene amounts of money— as if what he'd inherited hadn't been enough. He had since broadened his investments to become a billionaire at thirty-two.

His wealth and power cloaked him in authority and an air of earned arrogance, but she hadn't expected him to project so much sheer magnetism.

He was ridiculously handsome and compelling. His tuxedo didn't have to do any work, but its pleated shirt and white bow tie accentuated his tanned, clean-shaven jaw. His jacket was beautifully tailored to his wide shoulders, and the crisp trousers were neatly hemmed to drape a few inches past where his legs stopped above the knee.

His bone structure was to die for with his stern brow, sensual lips and heavy-lidded bedroom eyes. It was impossible to tell the color of his irises in the subdued lighting of the reception hall, but she knew them to be stormy gray.

She belatedly straightened while he continued to hold her dumbfounded stare, absently offering the tray to the group as he did.

Someone tittered about him missing his calling.

Freja was only dimly aware of the world beyond their sustained eye contact. Her heart was racing as though she'd run up ten flights of stairs. A flush of something like shyness or embarrassment was washing through her along with strange tugs and a tremendous sensual awareness throughout her entire body.

She tried to dismiss it as the silly vestiges of an infatuation that was so far in the past, it shouldn't affect her now. It hadn't even been *him* she'd had a pre-pubescent crush on!

That wasn't what this was, though. This was far more intense. Physical.

Was it *lust*? How mortifying.

He swiveled the empty tray back to her and cocked one eyebrow. "Do I know you?"

"No!" She nearly choked on her tongue. "I mean, I met y— I thought you were someone else." Not true, but her very brief history with his brother wasn't something she wanted to blurt out in front of strangers. Far too many questions followed when she spoke about her childhood.

"We've never met," she hurried to affirm in a sputter, but her discomfiture made him narrow his eyes. Butterflies invaded her stomach. "Have a nice evening."

She took the tray and walked away with a dizzy stagger. It took everything in her not to look back over her shoulder as she fetched more canapés and continued serving.

Nearly a full hour passed in which she tracked back and forth, waiting for everyone to filter into the ballroom and find their seats. She forced a smile and concentrated on not becoming clumsy when her limbs didn't feel as if they were her own.

Giovanni Catalano stayed on her radar the entire time.

Was it her imagination or was she on his? She didn't catch him looking at her, but she experienced the sensation of being observed.

She lost track of him once everyone had finally entered the ballroom, though. Still disconcerted, she busied herself with gathering abandoned napkins and dishes from the reception hall. The sense of being watched returned and she spun around.

His wheels had made his approach nearly silent, but there he was. An intense zing of electrical awareness went through her, so sharp it hurt.

"Come." He neatly pivoted and rolled down the hall.

Her heart lurched and she glanced to see the people in the ballroom were watching screens flashing to life with a presentation. Her colleagues would be looking for her to help serve shortly, but she could slip away unnoticed for a few minutes. Pulse racing unevenly, she followed.

Giovanni ducked down a corridor, turned the handle on a door, and led her into the empty cloakroom. A handful of light wraps and jackets hung on the racks, but the shutters were closed and the attendant absent.

He swiveled to confront her and nodded for her to close the door.

She did, still astonished to be in his presence.

"*Have* we met?" he demanded.

"No. I mean, I know who you are." Freja wished she'd kept her tray, needing a shield of some type. Not that she felt unsafe, but nor did she feel completely safe, either. Something about him struck her as dangerous in ways she couldn't articulate. Not that he wanted to hurt her, but she suspected he *could*. He was so muscled and had that air of power.

She was breathless in his presence for no

explicable reason, completely beyond her depth—which was odd for her. She rolled with punches and was almost always ten steps ahead of most people around her.

Nevertheless, she found herself sinking into the single wooden chair tucked beneath an empty section of a rack, weakened simply by the force of his personality.

A brief flicker of surprise went across his expression as she came down to his eye level.

"Why did you give those people the impression we've had sex?" he asked bluntly.

"I didn't. Did I?" She pressed into the hard rungs of the chair back. "No one thought that! Why would they?"

"They not only thought it, they judged me a cradle robber." His turbulent gaze took her in from crown to toes. "You're what? Twenty-two?"

"Twenty-three." Not a young twenty-three, either. At least, she knew a lot of people her age who were far less capable of looking after themselves. He made her feel positively juvenile, though. Like those perfectly sensible students who spouted feminist doctrines, then grew flushed and got all high-voiced around the football quarterback. "I'm really embarrassed for reacting like that." She fought to keep her voice steady and clear. "I didn't mean to."

"Why did you?" His demeanor was both compelling and faintly ominous. "Who did you think I was?"

"No one. Well… It was a prevarication. I knew right away that you're…" Oh, God, she was touching her hair. Playing with the fine hairs beneath her ponytail, where the hollow at the back of her neck was prickly with heightened awareness. Exactly like a flirty cheerleader. She clasped her hands in her lap. "I met your brother once. When I was a child."

His head went back and his whole body bunched as though preparing for a fight. His hands closed into fists and his jaw hardened.

She understood that reaction. It happened to her sometimes when people mentioned her father. Years of carrying grief didn't mean it no longer had the power to knock the wind out of you, especially when it arrived out of the blue.

"He made an impression," she continued gently, understanding, too, that there could be a gift hidden behind the sucker punch. A new memory could bring that person to life again, if only for a brief, intangible moment. "It was a fencing class for children."

"In Sicily?" Another raking glance filled with skepticism.

"I was there with my father. He often enrolled me in local activities while he worked. Stefano was teaching with a girl named Paloma."

Giovanni's head jerked slightly at the sound of his brother's name. He offered her a three-quarter profile under the unforgiving fluorescent light. "You would have been very young. Seven?" he calculated.

"He said I had potential." She smiled with nostalgia for the little girl who had developed instant hero worship from being noticed by such a dynamic young man. "I thought I would go on to become an Olympian like him."

His cheek ticked. "Did you?"

"No." Laughably, she wasn't much of anything, not even a proper US citizen. One day she might become a schoolteacher. At best she could call herself an author, but she wasn't even published yet and was riding on her father's coattails. "No, that swashbuckling fantasy went the way of my equally delusional dream that I would grow up and marry him."

His choked-off laugh could have been actual humor or a measure of outrage that she would dare to aspire to marry such a man.

"He was always flirting with Paloma during class," she explained. "He was so dashing and full of compliments, he became the ideal against which I judged all other boys when I grew old enough to have an interest in them. None had much chance after that." She sighed wistfully, laughing at herself before she sobered. "I was devastated when I heard he'd been killed. It was the first time I understood that people could die before their time."

He was staring holes through her, leaving hollow spaces, but she said what was in her because she knew she would regret it if she didn't take this chance to express her sincere condolences when she had this chance.

"He talked about you with fondness. I was worried about you after the accident. Sad for you losing your brother and your parents. I always wanted a sibling myself." She shrugged self-consciously at having such depth of compassion for a complete stranger. "I've looked you up over the years—which makes me sound like a stalker, I suppose, but I only viewed public things like your events at the games and read up on the apps you developed. That's why I recognized you and acted so strangely. I'm sorry I made you uncomfortable."

Uncomfortable? Giovanni snorted. He had thought his cover was blown.

Maybe it was. Freja—why had she only given him her first name?—was setting off all sorts of alarms on his internal gauges, from self-preservation to the sexual ones he did his best to ignore.

She was too beautiful to disregard out of hand, though, even in a cheap, ill-fitting catering uniform. Her black vest hugged her slender waist, emphasizing the thrust of her hips and breasts. She wasn't tall, but he'd watched her for an hour and she moved like a dancer, graceful and light. There wasn't a speck of makeup on her face, but her translucent skin looked soft and luminous as baby powder. Her lashes and brows were nearly invisible, glinting pale gold, same as the hair pulled back into a simple ponytail. Her blue eyes bloomed like cornflowers and her pale pink lips looked smooth as rose petals.

That impression of absolute innocence was an illusion, though. She possessed an underlying maturity that allowed her to hold his gaze with disconcerting confidence—and imbue their stare with a pulse of male-female awareness.

Proceed with caution, he warned himself, even as he rationalized that he had no choice but to proceed.

"Have dinner with me tomorrow."

She blinked, appearing startled by the invitation, which didn't line up with his apprehension that she had approached him for the sole purpose of nurturing a better acquaintance.

Her hesitation could also be an illusion, he reminded himself, but it caused a surprisingly brutal clench of disappointment in him. "No?"

"If I can switch my shift, yes," she said with a shy smile. "Thank you. I'd like that." She was looking at him much the way he was studying her. *Who is this person? I must find out.*

He couldn't allow her to see beneath his surface, of course, but oh, did he want to dig beneath hers. He took her number.

"I should get back," she said with a glance to the closed door, but she didn't rise. She studied him with an expectancy, as though she was waiting for something more.

To hell with it. The manufactured shell of

a persona he wore was necessary, but he was all man beneath. A nudge of his wheels and he was close enough to touch her. He didn't. Not yet. He managed to maintain some shred of self-control, but he wanted to. Unless...

"I'm not my brother."

"I know." Her brow quirked, dismissing the very idea. "That was a childish crush, not—"

He lifted his brows, confounded by her and fighting not to show it.

"Whatever this is." Her gaze searched his.

Yes, what was it? He wanted to know, too. He absently braked his wheels and dropped his hand on the edge of her chair. He felt the small jolt in her thigh against his inner wrist as he leaned in, waited a half second for her to decide if she wanted to reject him, then set his mouth against hers.

He'd been so focused on the job at hand for so long, he'd forgotten how satisfying it was to let himself feel. To *taste*. To experience the surprised tremble of a woman's lips. Hers were as smooth and soft as they looked, parting with welcome and moving in tentative response.

Hooks of desire snagged into him while a wind seemed to buffet them, making them sway. He lifted his free hand to her neck, drew her forward a fraction more so he could deepen their kiss, suddenly ravenous for all things sexual. For *her*. His blood became fire and she was the rain.

She made a noise that was pleasure and surrender, gorgeous and evocative. She leaned into him. One of her hands found his arm, the other touched his shoulder.

Without breaking their kiss, he gathered her and dragged her into his lap.

She gasped, eyes blinking open with surprise before her arms went around his shoulders. She set her mouth against his and made another of those blissful humming noises as her breasts mashed against his chest.

She was making this too easy. He knew that objectively, and he wasn't so desperate for female company that he took it where he found it. He shouldn't allow this seemingly unfettered response of hers to fuel his, but he was racing past normal checkpoints. In another instinctive move, he dug his fingers into her hip and pressed her deeper into the cradle of his thighs, wanting the weight and pressure of her in the places he could feel it.

Her hands went into his hair as if she knew how sensitive his scalp was. The tingle of pleasure was so acute, he had to bite back a ragged groan. He buried the sound in her throat as he ran his mouth down to her collar, suddenly starving, wanting all of her, right here, right now.

A pair of women walked past the far side of the vented panel that was the only thing hiding them from view. Their gossipy voices yanked him back to an awareness that he and Freja were essentially in public.

She stared at him the way a stranger might who had blindly stepped in front of his car, her whole life flashing in her eyes while her shiny lips quivered in astonishment that she was still intact.

He felt the same, which was sobering enough to steady his galloping heart.

"Tomorrow," he promised, forcing himself to remember that she might be a plant. He helped her to her feet, determined to use the time between now and then to find out.

And even though he would need every minute of that time to assess whether he could trust her, he was already urging that time to pass quickly.

Freja walked briskly to the Manhattan restaurant from the gallery where she'd been working a few blocks away.

Her catering uniform was in a bag over her shoulder. She had already changed into a tweed skirt over knee-high boots with red leggings and a red turtleneck. She'd topped it with a brown motorcycle jacket mined from a thrift store. When she had combed out her hair, it had immediately lost the waves she'd hoped to retain by keeping it in a plait all day. No such luck. As always, it was fine as spider silk and arrow-straight. She had plopped a newsboy cap over it and called it "good enough."

The busy street was carpeted in cherry blossom petals from the trees that lined it. It made a snowy carpet for Giovanni where he had parked his chair beside the wrought iron rail that surrounded a massive oak. He was reading something on his phone. The collar of his white shirt poked from his gray pullover, and the end of a pale blue scarf flicked in the breeze like the tip of a cat's tail. He was casual and stunningly elegant, definitely not wearing anything that had been purchased secondhand.

Both road and foot traffic were heavy and noisy, but he lifted his head and looked straight at her as she approached, as though he'd been aware of her from the moment she turned the corner at the end of the block. His black hair was charmingly ruffled by the breeze, his tanned face naturally stern, yet lit with probing curiosity.

"You've written a book," was his cryptic greeting. "It's very compelling."

"How—"

She cut herself off as he lifted a hand, leaving her in the awkward position of rebuffing his invitation to embrace and kiss in greeting or bend to accept it. She'd been reliving last night's kiss nonstop, so she set her hand on his shoulder and leaned in.

Something flashed in his gray eyes—humor, surprise—then an inferno of heat before he steadied her with one hard arm and captured her mouth with startling greed. Her heart leaped and her feet seemed to leave the ground. All of her felt suspended and floating as she abandoned herself to the wonder that was his mouth playing over hers.

She could have kissed him forever, here in the street, while strangers brushed by them. *He* was a stranger, she reminded herself distantly, but he didn't feel like one. She felt as though he'd been calling to her for her entire life and she had finally caught up to him.

He let their kiss dwindle to a series of

briefer tastes while a rumble of deprivation sounded in his throat. He kept her hand in his own as she straightened. She locked her soggy knees, trying to remain upright.

"I was offering to take your bag, but thank you." His mouth curved with amusement, while his heavy eyelids transmitted a smoldering beam of sensual appreciation. "I've been thinking about you and wanted to do that again."

"Oh, my God." She ducked her brow behind her free hand, flustered at having read the situation so wrongly.

He released a soft chuckle across her knuckles and kissed the back of her hand. "Give me your bag and we'll get out of this wind."

She slid her bag from her shoulder and set it in his lap, then obeyed his wave that invited her to walk down the ramp ahead of him. Inside, he passed her bag to the maître d' and she gave up her jacket before they were shown through the intimate dining lounge.

From the outside, with its small street-level windows, she had presumed this was a mid-range Italian restaurant. It was far more impressive and exclusive. Subtle lighting lent intimacy to the sumptuous furniture arranged in private pockets and alcoves. A harpist in the middle of the room plucked a soothing mood into the air. A woman in a corner wore an epoch's worth of diamonds, while the man sampling wine was a famous American with a full complement of EGOT awards. His companion was a well-known human rights lawyer.

"Am I dressed all right?" Freja asked in a whisper.

"You're perfect," he assured her.

Moments later they were settled at a discreet table. His chair was armless and streamlined, but still too bulky for the space on the opposite side of the table. He slid into the spot on the side, close enough that only the corner of the table separated them.

She self-consciously set aside her cap and dropped her phone into it, then flicked her hair behind her shoulders, aware of him watching her as he ordered a bottle of wine.

When they were alone, she cleared her throat and said, "I was going to ask how you learned about my book." She'd only given him her first name yesterday, partly because it tended to prompt the conversation she could feel building right now. "I'm even more interested in how you have a copy? It doesn't come out until the fall."

"I'm extremely well-connected." His mouth quirked as though that was an understatement. "I received it an hour ago, so I haven't read all of it. You're still in Mongolia. My sense is that it gets worse before it gets better." He grew somber.

Various accounts of her story had been excerpted in the news when she was first freed. Throughout her recent four years at university, while writing the book, she had read aloud sections in class or circulated them for feedback. She was used to a reaction of sheer disbelief or dismay that she wasn't more disparaging of the people who'd held her.

Giovanni only waited patiently for her to respond.

"I think we've established that loss is as bad as it gets," she murmured.

"True," he agreed in a grave tone. "Is that why you wanted to write it? As an homage to your father? I'd heard of him, but only vaguely as a travel writer. I had no idea he'd been such an avid blogger. And so political."

Something in that leading statement caused her a brief flashback to those early days of arriving in America, when government types had interrogated her incessantly. Giovanni was the son of an ambassador, she reminded herself. His interest was likely ingrained from his early life observing the highest level of world governments, not suspicion that she was a cog in such things.

"Pappa didn't take sides so much as document blatant injustice when he came across it. His true interest was culture and history and the beauty of nature that we too often overlook. That's what his fans wanted from him—escape from the clamor and nonsense of their own lives into the reassurance that we're all part of the same human fabric. And yes, there was a part of me that wanted to give his readers his final chapter. They did, after all, pay for my upkeep most of my life."

They still did. Many of his books had gone into reprint after the story of his death broke. She was his sole beneficiary.

"I imagine they feel invested in you, being his companion through all his adventures."

"You'll laugh, but I honestly had no idea how famous he was. My publisher told me to join social media to promote my book, and my phone exploded. I hadn't even read any of his books cover to cover until I was at university. Why would I need to? I was there. And in the places we visited, he was only seen as a nosy tourist."

His attention was fully on her as though he examined and weighed every word she spoke. It was disconcerting, causing her to blush with self-consciousness.

"Now that I've started my own blog, and realize how much work it is to find interesting content, I realize why he exploited me so shamelessly."

"Does that bother you?"

"Not really. He was always very good about asking which photos he could post or whether he could quote something I'd said. He would flag pages in his manuscript and let me veto anything I felt was too personal or didn't reflect well on me. I rarely pushed back because it never occurred to me that people even read what he wrote or cared about me. At best, I imagined they were reading for snippets of history and odd mishaps like arguing with a donkey on a muddy track. I didn't realize they came to believe they knew me, not until I was brought to America and the reporters wouldn't leave me alone."

"Why America? You're Swedish, aren't you?" Again, she had the flickering sense she was being debriefed, but this was how her life had gone since her father's death. Her notoriety gave people the impression they had a right to ask personal questions.

"I have distant relations in Sweden, but we only returned to renew our passports. My mother died when I was four and my father took me with him on his travels."

"He educated you himself?"

"He was a teacher in a previous life." She nodded. "He enrolled me in local schools at different times, mostly for language and socialization. You must know a little about that sort of upbringing?" She tried to bat the conversation in his direction.

"I do," he said after the briefest of pauses. "While my father was alive, we lived wherever he happened to be assigned. I resented being uprooted every year, forced to say goodbye to my latest batch of friends, then having to assimilate into a new culture. Above anything, I wanted to stay in one place. Be careful what you wish for," he said with an ironic nod at his chair.

"Is New York your home now?"

"My complex business interests keep me traveling. I have many homes."

"You've become your father," she teased.

"It appears that way." He said it lightly, but his face smoothed to unreadable and he sat back, popping the fragile bubble of connection they'd briefly shared.

The wine arrived, distracting her from examining her distinct impression that he didn't want to talk about himself. Giovanni ordered appetizers and they clinked glasses.

"How did you come to settle in New York instead of Sweden? School?"

"You could read the book to learn all this. You didn't have to buy me dinner," she pointed out.

"I want the raw data, not the polished prose. Unless you'd rather not talk about it?" That penetrating gaze of his made her heart stall each time it landed on her. There seemed to be a degree of challenge in it, as though refusing to talk would be seen as a sign of weakness or guilt.

"I don't mind," she lied.

She'd told her story enough times it was something she could usually do while holding herself at a distance so the facts didn't hurt too much to revisit. With him, however, her typical confidence was butting up against a level of self-assurance she had never encountered. She felt overpowered, which made her defenses shaky. She had to remind herself that she didn't need his approval for any reason, but it didn't stop her from wanting it and she didn't understand why.

"You might have seen in the book's acknowledgment the mention of my father's editor? Oliver was instrumental in getting me out of North Korea. It's why the US took over negotiations from the Swedish officials. Oliver worked tirelessly for two years to learn whether I was alive, locate exactly where I was, and petition for my release. He brought me into his home afterward."

"Because he felt responsible for sending you and your father there?"

"It was my father's choice to go. No, Oliver regarded himself as a surrogate father after such a long friendship with Pappa. He and his wife, Barbara, continue to be very kind to me, but I was nineteen when I arrived. I didn't want to be a foster child or a houseguest." Not again. "I had several offers for ghostwriters to tell my story, but Oliver suggested I write the book myself, as part of a creative writing degree. I had some money from my father's estate for tuition, Oliver made some calls to his alma mater. I thought university would be a good way to integrate into Western society, that I would meet people my age and expand my mental horizons."

"Oh? How did that go?" Giovanni's mouth pursed knowingly. "I'm guessing your horizons were already stratospheres beyond your peers."

"Pizza, sex, binge drinking... That's all they cared about." She sighed. "The people who had traveled hadn't really traveled. They had spent summers on a yacht in the Greek islands or went on a spring break rager through the Caribbean. Even my instructors seemed stunted, hammering at me to draw a thicker line between black and white. They couldn't understand why I wasn't angrier. *They* made me angry, trying to force me to rewrite my own experience to fit the narrative they thought it should have."

"It's a sensational story. Why wouldn't you sensationalize it for profit?"

"Exactly. I couldn't possibly have affection for the people who had held me. That would make them *people*."

She waited for the questions that usually came when she got this far, the ones that probed for salacious details. Had she been mistreated or assaulted? What horrible things had she done to survive?

"Were you not given an advance for your book? Why are you working in catering?"

That almost sounded as though he was

more interested in how she'd come to meet him at the hotel last night than how she'd been pried from the clutches of a notoriously uncooperative government.

"I used my advance as a down payment on a small flat, but I have a mortgage and living expenses. Oddly enough, a creative writing degree isn't at the top of HR managers' wish lists." She shrugged. "So I tutor ESL students, and a friend got me in with this catering company. Once I get my book tour out of the way, I'll start a teacher certification program."

"You want to shape young minds?"

"Open them, at least." She made a more determined effort to steer the conversation in his direction. "May I ask you a question?"

"Never married and currently uninvolved," he said promptly, maintaining his intense stare, though it held a shadow of self-deprecation at what he was implying.

"I wish I could say the same," she threw back, deadpan.

His face abruptly fell with shocked dismay.

She burst out laughing.

"I didn't expect you to be so gullible." Freja's laugh was so merry, her expression so incandescent, he was spellbound.

Giovanni's only thought should have been to question how his team had missed something as vital as romantic associations, but her remark had prompted a far more visceral reaction. Involved? *No.* He wanted her for himself.

Which was not only an uncharacteristic thrust of unjustified jealousy, it was the sort of emotional reaction he had trained himself not to have. The fact she had so easily slid past his well-fortified shields against any sort of manipulations, intended or otherwise, told him exactly how dangerous she was.

He tried to neutralize all of that firepower of hers with some heat of his own.

"You're nothing like I expected." He picked up her hand and brought it to his mouth to drop a kiss in her palm. "Which is why I have such a strong disinclination to share you."

She blushed, and he felt her hand twitch in nervous reaction, but she left it trustingly in his. Her brow pulled into a small frown. "You're possessive?"

"I'm Sicilian, *bidduzza.* I'm incapable of being anything else."

Each breath he drew was laden with the scent of her—spring and berries and something sweet like almond cookies. He wanted to continue nuzzling along her wrist, but contented himself with tracing his thumb along her love line.

This isn't real, a voice in his head reminded him. She might not be as innocent as she projected. Even more concerning, she might be, in which case he definitely shouldn't allow himself to sink into any sort of involvement with her.

How was he to know either way if he didn't spend time with her, though? It was a convenient rationalization for pursuing a woman he couldn't have. What the hell was he going to do?

"What was your real question?" he prompted, still caressing her palm with his thumb.

"Do you still fence?"

Ah, yes. He had confirmed that small detail, at least. An online search had unearthed a passage from one of Hugo Anderson's earliest books about his "young companion," as her father had referred to her, taking fencing lessons from an Olympic hopeful. For weeks after, every stray piece of driftwood had become a weapon until a nasty sliver had forced her to find other amusements.

"These days I stay fit in ways that allow me

to watch the market numbers or take a conference call. Fencing requires complete focus."

"And world domination via cell phone apps doesn't?"

"That was dumb luck," he said with uncharacteristic frankness—and a hint of disparagement that she leaped on with an incisive frown.

"What do you do with your downtime, then? Inspire me. My pastimes are all very tame."

He scratched his cheek, stalling. "You don't yearn to fill your time with the obvious? Marriage and a family?"

She let her mouth hang open before she accused, "Sexist."

"How is that sexist? Many people want those things, gender notwithstanding."

"Do you?"

She wasn't afraid to put him on the spot. It was as annoying as it was refreshing. Given his wealth and position, most people jumped at his every whim, rarely challenging him on his opinions or what he did with his life.

His response to her question should have been a quick and firm no. He'd buried any youthful assumptions that he would one day have a family when he'd buried the one he'd had. Part of that reaction had been bitterness. Lately it was simply a matter of priorities. Close relationships of any kind were a vulnerability he couldn't afford.

But he had a sudden vision of her in his bed, gaze sleepy and filled with infinite possibilities. His heart lurched in warning. Or was it masculine craving?

"Marriage isn't a priority for me," he said in an implacable signal. "I've always been focused on other things. My physical health, athletic training, my education. My investments." Not to mention unraveling multinational conspiracies and political corruptions without getting himself further maimed or killed in the process.

"Same." She nodded thoughtfully. "I've been focused on my book and finding my feet. In many ways, I feel as though I'm still waiting for my life to start." She looked at the hand still in his warm grip. "This is the first date I've been on in ages. The handful of friends I made at school have moved on to careers and other things. I know a lot of people, but I've always moved around so much, I've never connected deeply with anyone."

Her thumb tentatively caressed the backs of his fingers. His hair damned near stood on end, the sensation caused such an acute reaction in him.

At the same time, the wistful yearning in her voice reverberated off the steel shields he'd erected around his heart, making her words echo inside him as though they were his own. He had an overpowering urge to mute that inner vibration with the press of her body against his.

All his good sense flew out the window. Before he realized what he was saying, his voice rumbled from the depths of his chest.

"Come home with me."

"Now?" Her pupils dilated and a visible quake went through her, one that leaped so quickly onto the suggestion, his honed instincts of self-preservation tingled in warning, but a responsive ripple of pleasure rolled through him. How could he resist her when this was how they reacted to one another?

Don't let her see how desperate you are, he cautioned himself.

While his mouth affirmed, "Right now."

CHAPTER TWO

"THIS IS SOMETHING I'm still getting used to," Freja admitted nervously as they left the elevator into his penthouse. Recessed lighting kept the lounge dim enough that the view of the city lights was like a carpet of stars beyond the darkened windows. She trailed her hand over the buttery leather of the overstuffed sofa. "I thought Oliver and Barbara lived like kings in their two-bedroom walkup. This…"

There were no words for the kind of expansive luxury surrounding her. Until moving to New York, she'd only seen this sort of wealth in historic palaces. Catering had sent her into a few high-end hotels and penthouses, but even those paled next to what appeared to be a mansion atop a skyscraper. The floors were a gleaming hardwood, the drapes silk, the art on the walls a colorful mix of modern impressionists. Beyond the value in such things, the real luxury was in how the entire space was tastefully customized for a man who moved in a wheelchair instead of on two feet.

Something introspective shadowed his expression as he hung her jacket. He paused.

"When I asked you here, I was only thinking that I wanted to be alone with you. I didn't consider the way you've been forced to live in the past." His mouth pulled with consternation. "If you have second thoughts—I hope you feel comfortable here, but leave anytime if you don't. Or we can go back to the restaurant." He turned to regard her as though she were a complex puzzle he was trying to solve.

"I like to believe I'm a good judge of character."

She had believed it until meeting him, at least. He was hard to read, though. She continued to finger the soft leather of the sofa, soothed by its texture as she considered his contradictions. Bold enough to state what he wanted, compassionate enough to anticipate her hidden apprehensions. Open about his attraction, completely closed off in other ways.

"I wouldn't have come here if I thought you were planning to attack me."

His expression eased into a smoldering one

that pulled her insides tight with anticipation. "Only in a very sensual sense, *bidduzza*. And with your explicit consent, of course." He rolled forward. "Come. Sit," he invited, nodding at the sofa.

She hesitated behind it.

His expression cleared, but his mouth tightened briefly. "That's fine," he said evenly. "I presumed you'd have questions."

"I do, but not— Well, that too, I guess." She hadn't even considered whether he had full sexual function, only thinking that she wanted to be alone with him, too. "It's more…" She could hear herself stammering and wanted to die of mortification. "I've never done this," she blurted.

His shoulders relaxed and one of his dark eyebrows lifted in self-deprecation. "This is considerably faster than I usually move, myself."

"No, I mean…" She nervously linked her hands before her. "I've never had sex."

His head went back in astonishment.

She wrinkled her nose. "I knew you'd think I'm odd." Her fellow students had. "That's why I mentioned it."

"It's not odd." He tilted his head, conceding, "Okay, I'm surprised. I didn't expect someone as worldly as you are wouldn't have taken a lover somewhere along the line." He studied her again in that way that picked over her bones, but left small fires in its wake.

She was used to being a curiosity. People disbelieved things she said about herself and her life. For the most part she didn't care what others thought of her, but Giovanni's skepticism was different. That shadow of doubt he wore provoked a small outrage in her along with a clench of something more defensive. She wanted him to see her exactly as she was. To know her and like her and want her despite all the nicks and dents that life had left upon her.

"There wasn't at least one young man at university who tempted you?"

"They all seemed very one-track and immature." The one she had thought had potential turned out to play for another team. She shrugged self-consciously. "No one made me feel like I wanted more than coffee and kisses."

"But I do?" His face was impassive while the line of his shoulders had turned to granite.

"Why is that hard to believe? You invited me here. I thought that meant we were mutually attracted." She crossed her arms protectively.

"I'm very attracted to you," he assured her in a voice that curled her toes in her boots. "It's still a big step for you to take with someone you barely know."

She hunched her shoulders to her ears. "Growing up the way I did, always moving to a new place, I learned that I don't often get second chances. If there was a place I wanted to see or something I wanted to do, I had to take the opportunity when it was presented or we would be in the next town or across a border and I couldn't go back."

"I'm a unique experience you don't want to miss?" His voice chilled with warning.

"Am I not for you?" she asked with a spark of tetchiness. "Because if I'm a run-of-the-mill hookup, then yes, I would prefer to take my jacket and bag and find my own way home."

His cheeks hollowed and his mouth pursed in doleful humor. "You're definitely unique, Freja." He absently ran the backs of his fingers under the angle of his jaw.

The silence drew out until her stomach was so tight she could hardly breathe. She looked to her bag where he'd set it on the table by the door.

"I'm trying to make myself say that this isn't your only opportunity to sleep with me," he said in a voice that went gritty and thick. "I know I should tell you that if you're feeling pressured, we can back off. We can date and wait for a time that feels right." He shook his head, jaw clenched. "But I'll be leaving for Europe next week. Which is another reason you should be sensible about this decision. I'll be there through the summer, possibly longer. I wouldn't expect you to wait for me."

And wouldn't invite her to come with him. He was warning her this wasn't the beginning of anything serious. She absorbed that as a clash that rang through her whole body. But as she weighed little against nothing, there was no contest. She would take what she could get.

"If you want to leave, go. I'll call you tomorrow. If you want to stay the night, then I want you in my bed."

That declaration was as weighty as a thick wool quilt, a little abrasive, but strangely comforting. She warmed under it. Fast.

"I want to stay." Even though her stomach

was nothing but butterflies in anticipation. "That's why I'm here."

His breath left him in a jagged laugh. "That frankness of yours is going to be the death of me. Come here." In a well-practiced shift, he used the arm of the sofa to transfer himself onto the cushions. He held out a hand to her.

She came around and let him draw her to sit next to him. He set one arm along the back of the sofa and angled toward her. His light touch encouraged her to angle toward him and drape her legs across his thighs.

"You won't hurt me," he assured her, but it was the way his touch played across her knees that made her twitch in reaction. He pointed to what was left of his right leg. "This one is completely without sensation. I can't control it at all. Sometimes it spasms. This one I can move a bit and feel some pressure, but no heat or pain." He thwacked his finger against his meatier left thigh. "I don't feel anything at all right here." He drew a wide band from his spine around his rib cage to the middle of his chest on the right side. "Sensation is patchy through here." He waved his hand over his abdomen and lap. "If I move your hand when you're touching me, that's why." He picked up her hand and played with her fingers. "Go ahead and do the same with me. I want to touch you where you enjoy it most."

Her fingers flexed in reaction at the idea of setting his hand in intimate places.

The corners of his mouth deepened knowingly. He set a tiny kiss on her knuckle, melting her thought processes one brain cell at a time.

"My shoulders and scalp and earlobes are really sensitive. My left nipple." He shrugged at that incongruity. "I may not finish the way you expect. Don't take that as a reflection on you or my level of enjoyment."

"I don't know what to expect," she reminded him, trying to keep the moment light while she quaked internally at the enormity of what they were discussing so calmly and naturally.

"Right. I should have said, everything that happens between us is a completely typical experience exactly as you would have had with your able-bodied university nits."

She chuckled dryly, but her smile faded as he trailed his reverent gaze over her face.

"Or not." He picked up a tendril of her hair, letting it sift through his fingers. "That is sleek as a satin ribbon, isn't it? I've been dying to know." He did it again. "Smooth and cool. Like you," he added in a tone that maybe was supposed to be whimsical, but she was having trouble tracking.

Her scalp grew sensitized and a shiver chased down her spine. She reflexively pulled from his light hold on her hand to cross her arms and rub away the goose bumps that rose beneath her sleeves.

"Am I making you shiver? I want to." He stroked a light touch from her shoulder to her elbow and back, reigniting the prickling sensation she'd tried to erase. His touch firmed into a warm massage that was equally inciting. "Don't hold back any of your reactions. Your pleasure is my pleasure."

"Really?" Her experience with men was… not that. More like, *Go farther, faster. Why aren't you into this?*

"I want to know you're as excited as I am." He tucked her hair behind her ear and played his fingertip along the whorls he exposed, caressing behind and into the hollow beneath her earlobe.

Why that made her nipples stand up, she didn't know, but she felt them tighten and sting. She bit her lip and wanted to lift her hand to erase that sensation, too, especially when his gaze dropped. She looked down and yes, her nipples were poking against the soft red knit of her pullover.

"I want it to be so good, you can't bring yourself to leave my bed." His voice grew husky and intimate, his concentration wholly on the vision he created as he slid his hand to her side. He pressed the knit of her turtleneck taut so her breast was blatantly outlined, nipple standing firmly against it. "No bra?"

"I don't like them," she confessed faintly.

"Neither do I. Not anymore."

She had never experienced such a strange euphoria simply by being near someone, barely touching. His light caress through her clothing was feathery and wonderful. She liked being snuggled close to his solid warmth, able to discern his strength and take in his scent of wool and outdoors and faint aftershave and a more intimate, personal fragrance that was spicy and musky and all him.

His touch slid back to her shoulder, encouraging her to lean in as he did, closer and closer, gaze on his mouth. He didn't kiss her, though. He touched light kisses along her jaw, then stole a very brief kiss. Started to come back for more.

She drew back slightly. "Shouldn't we go to the bedroom?"

He frowned with insult. "I'll have to turn in my Italian citizenship if I don't seduce you."

"But I already said yes."

"You agreed to the sensual attack I promised you." He grew serious. Maybe faintly suspicious. "Why the hurry?"

"I'm nervous," she admitted with a sheepish wrinkle of her nose.

"Then we should take it slow."

"But I feel…impatient." Her low-grade blush increased until she was so hot, she probably glowed, fully embarrassed by how urgent she felt. "I want to be naked and feel all of you and know how it will be when we're… together."

He gathered her in his strong arms and his chest muscles flexed as he pulled her to sit fully in his lap, so they were nose to nose. His big hands moved over her lower back and hips, waking her up to swirling sensations that expanded into her inner thighs.

"This is how it will be," he told her, opening his mouth against her throat and licking at her flesh. "Better and better with every minute that goes by."

He really did attack her senses. She caught her breath at the onslaught of sensations, gasping when his hands hardened on her, holding her in place.

"I'm dying to have you naked and spread out on my bed, weak with need for the release I give you." His hot breath wafted against her nape. "I'm going to take liberties that are liable to shock you. I'm as impatient as you are for all of that."

"Are you?" He seemed in such complete control.

"Do *you* lack sensation below the waist? What do you think that is against your ass? A penknife?"

She chuckled shyly and glanced down to where a stiff ridge dug into her cheek. She gave a small wriggle that made heat flare in his eyes.

Oh.

She did it again, testing her newfound feminine power.

"You *will* be the death of me," he said in a rasp and rocked to shift his legs open a little farther, nestling her deeper into his lap. "Can we lose these?" He tugged the zipper on the inside of her boot.

She nodded, wondering how the slow relaxing of her boots and their loose drop could pull such an erotic sensation from her loins to the arch of her foot.

He caressed her calf and invited, "Kiss me."

She did, sliding her arms around his neck while she worked her mouth over his, dabbing her tongue into the taste of him between his parted lips. Trying to slake a greedy hunger she'd never experienced—or expressed—in her life.

Gradually, she became aware of his arms firming around her. His hand was in her hair, his other one soothing along her rib cage while he took control of their kiss. He was unhurried about it, but she slowly became aware that they were fully involved. He was thoroughly ravaging her and it was *fantastic*. She curled into him with a groan, pressing her thighs together to ease the growing ache between them. When his touch crept over her breast and he molded the swell while sweeping his thumb across her nipple, she moaned into his mouth.

He drew back and his heavy-lidded gaze was fixated on where he was fondling her. "Let me see," he said in a thick voice and gave a tug against the back of the turtleneck.

"Yes, I'm so hot," she breathed anxiously.

"Me, too." He swept off his own pull-over first, then helped her do the same. He swore as she twisted her naked torso back toward him, stalling her with his wide hands against her shoulders, still balancing her on his thighs.

"You're so beautiful." His palms went down to cup the sides of her breasts. His thumbs shaped the swells to plump them and tilt her beaded nipples higher.

She trembled as she tried to work his shirt buttons loose. It wasn't easy. He dropped his head to set the sweetest kisses across her shoulders. His light touch grazed her stomach and ribs and tickled the curves of her breasts. It was such a tease! Her breasts grew heavy with anticipation. Everything in her wanted to sit still for the lovely sensations he was causing with those clever fingers and damp lips, but more than that, she wanted to *feel* him. His hair against her jaw made her turn her nose in to his scent, but she finally had his shirt undone enough to push it open and—"Oh!"

She thrust her arms beneath the edges, hugging his sides. The scrape of her naked breasts against the silken hairs on his chest sent a glorious, electrical excitement through her. He made a growling noise and caught her into a passionate kiss. As they devoured each other, tongues tangling, they moved against one another, skin against skin in hedonistic friction.

It took her a moment to realize her perception of falling was real. He was tipping her onto her back on the cushions, but coming down with her. He leaned over her, mouth finding her throat and taking soft, wet bites.

"Giovanni," she moaned.

"Say it like you mean it." His expression was so stark and intensely masculine, it should have been intimidating, but his touch as he cupped her breast was reverent. He looked at her naked flesh, licked at her nipple, then blew softly. Her loins pulsed in reaction.

"Giovanni," she said with all the yearning in her, tone ringing with plea and command.

He rewarded her with a delicate suction that had her tangling her fingers in his hair, arching up to offer more. She was going insane, she was so aroused, but he moved from one breast to the other and back until instinct drove her to slither herself more completely beneath him. Her body screamed for the weight of his. For his thighs between her own.

As they rearranged themselves, her skirt

rode up, allowing her to bend her knees on either side of his hips.

He balanced on one elbow over her. "Tell me if I'm too heavy."

"I like it." She pulled his shirt from his waistband and slid her palms all over his back.

He had the torso of a power lifter, thick chest and shoulder muscles rippling under her touch. When her fingers grazed his left nipple, he sucked in a sharp breath.

She lifted her hand. "Hurt?"

"No," he said on a jagged laugh. "It feels really good."

She touched him again, watching his eyes drift shut as she very deliberately played her thumbs across his nipples. His breathing grew uneven and her own arousal intensified as she watched the way he was reacting.

He suddenly snapped his eyes open and dragged her hand to his shoulder. "I'm going to lose it if you keep that up. Ladies first." He kissed her parted lips and settled his weight on her.

When she felt the pressure of his erection through their clothes against the juncture of her thighs, she tilted her hips to increase the pressure.

"What do you need?" He rolled onto his elbow and pressed the heat of his palm against her mound. "This?" He rocked his palm firmly.

"Yes," she moaned in anguished relief. "Was I hurting you?"

"Quit asking that." He nipped at the edge of her jaw. "The only thing that's hurting me is that I can't feel more of you." He searched beneath her skirt for the waistband of her leggings and worked his hand inside, fingers cleverly getting into her underwear.

He watched her expression as he did. She bit her lip, shy, yet dying of anticipation. She never let men get this far. It had never felt right, but now she dearly wanted to know how it would feel.

One long touch parted the wet seam of her folds, intimate and lovely. He returned to the swollen bundle of nerves he'd only grazed, as if he'd known exactly what he was doing all along. One firm circle and such an exquisite streak of pleasure went through her, she clenched her eyes shut to savor it while a decadent groan filled her throat.

"Hurt?" he mocked with a hot chuckle of his breath against her cheek. He did it again.

She groaned again and met his kiss with

a flagrant offer of her tongue while she rocked her hips to match the slow rhythm of his touch firming and gliding away, returning and easing, dipping lower and deeper, invading so that she clung to him with all her might, driven by sheer desire to cast off propriety and seek the pinnacle that suddenly loomed.

And there it was, quick and sweet and expansive, bathing her in a rush of tingles while her cries of satisfaction were muffled by his carnal kiss.

His touch stayed under her skirt, but eased to a proprietary hand on her belly while he let her break their kiss and catch her breath.

"You very nearly took me with you. That was incredibly sexy." He circled the tip of his nose against her own, kissed her temple, then her cheekbone. Through her haze, she thought he might be shaking.

She wished he had climaxed with her. She'd never orgasmed with anyone else in the room and she felt incredibly vulnerable right now, having done it by his hand. Letting him draw that from her gave him a power over her that she didn't know how to take back. He had broken down barriers in her before she fully understood how much protection they offered.

Even knowing that, however, latent desire throbbed in her blood. She was still aroused. She wanted more and the depth of want in her—for more of his touch, his kisses, and the pleasure he gave her—was genuinely painful. Her need for him felt as basic as breathing or eating. It was unsettling to become so carnal within the space of a few minutes.

"*Now* I want to go to the bedroom," he informed her smokily, setting one short, suggestive kiss on her mouth.

Her lips clung to his and she felt obvious in her desire. As though he knew her better than she knew herself. As though a single feel-up on the sofa had turned her into a slave to the lure of his touch.

Which it had. Her legs barely worked and she wound up in his lap, kissing his jaw and neck as he bumped them down the hall into the master bedroom.

One lamp glowed next to a huge, low bed. The floor-to-ceiling drapes had been drawn shut, but judging by the two walls of them, the entire corner was nothing but glass overlooking the city.

He nodded for her to sit on the bed while

he opened the drawer of the nightstand to withdraw condoms. "I don't ejaculate, but I always wear one."

She perched nervously and watched as he threw off his shirt and moved onto the mattress beside her. He dropped back and opened his fly, worked his pants off and pushed them to the floor. Then he stayed propped on his elbows, letting her look her fill.

She tracked her gaze from his alert expression to his powerful shoulders and flexed biceps to his flat abs. There was a distinct tan line above the band of his snug blue briefs. His erection pressed a line against it. Below that, his thighs were visibly different sizes, the right one thinner and amputated higher than the left. There was more scarring on the right one, too, and a nasty bruise.

"What happened?" she asked with concern, gently touching the blue-green smudge.

He glanced and dismissed it with, "I stumbled during gait therapy."

"You can walk?"

"I can balance on crutches and one prosthetic leg while dragging the other. It's not practical for daily life, but it keeps my good leg from atrophying and helps with other functions." He settled onto his back, one arm curled behind his head to reveal the tuft of hair beneath. He angled his head to study her. "I'm regretting taking off your boots. I would love to see your foot right here while you unzipped it." He patted the mattress next to his hip.

If he was feeling a fraction of the self-consciousness she was experiencing, there was no evidence of it. He radiated confidence and patience.

She stood, but she was so befuddled, her fingers couldn't find the zipper on her skirt.

"Please don't laugh at how awkward I am." She turned the skirt. Her hair fell across her face, blinding her as she tried to work the catch free.

"On the contrary, I'm turned on by the fact you're as excited as I am. Let me help." He pushed to sit up and she nervously edged closer. With no clumsiness whatsoever, he opened her skirt and brushed it off her hips.

He brought her twitching hands to his shoulders and pressed one palm to his neck so she could feel the rapid slam of his pulse. "I'm so aroused, I can hardly breathe."

His skin was faintly damp with perspiration, his nostrils flared and tense.

Yet he was in complete control. She stroked

her fingers through his hair, as though she'd been given the gift of petting a tiger. The strength and power in him awed her and the flare of excitement in his eyes excited her. It was reassuring to know he was reacting so strongly. Heady. He began to roll her leggings down and she pushed her panties off with them, kicking them away as she stood before him, still nervous, but driven by that urgency again.

A primordial noise rumbled in his chest as he looked at the thatch of blond over her mound. His splayed hands grasped her hips and drew big circles to her butt cheeks and the backs of her thighs, nudging her closer to the edge of the bed between his open thighs until her knees and shins rested against the side of the mattress. His hands lingered to caress in slow circles that were driving her mad while he blew softly on her curls.

A helpless noise left her and she dug her fingernails into his shoulders. Her inner muscles clenched while the rest of her went taut.

"Shy?" He dragged his gaze upward as if it took supreme effort. "Or something more?"

"Shy," she managed in a paper-thin voice. "I've never— No one—"

He set a light kiss against her mound and

she forgot how words worked. Every single nerve ending throughout her body pulsated.

He was a ridiculously patient man, teasing her with another small kiss into the crease where her thigh met her pelvis, then the other side. When his tongue traced a barely-there caress along the seam of her folds, skating a not-quite-fulfilling touch across the bud swollen with yearning, she moaned his name. Her fingers moved mindlessly in his hair.

He groaned and heat enveloped her flesh. She had thought what they'd done on the sofa was a type of paradise she could never again live without, but *this*. This was the sort of rapture that would induce her to do nearly anything to keep experiencing it.

He proved it, too. Just as the last vestiges of control were abandoning her, when she was so aroused she was relying on the hard hands under her butt to keep her upright while she pushed her hips into his lascivious kiss, he dropped his head back to look at her from beneath heavy eyelids.

An unconscious noise of loss throbbed in her throat.

He smiled, wicked and dark, then twisted to throw pillows into a pile against the headboard. He dragged himself to sit against them and met her gaze as he rocked to get his briefs down, revealing his thick erection. He took himself in hand, squeezed.

"You're going to decide how much you can take." He sounded as primal as she felt. He unwrapped a condom and rolled it on. "I can still feel heat. Pressure. Let me feel how hot and tight you are."

He invited her to straddle his thighs. There was no modesty as she splayed her knees on either side of his hips, but given what he'd done to her already, inhibitions were moot. He held himself steady for her to position herself and she began accepting him into her. It was deliberate and overwhelming, both physically and emotionally, but she had never wanted anything so much in her life.

The pinch of his broad shape entering her was sharp enough to startle her. She steadied herself by gripping the headboard.

"Take your time." His voice was gruff, his skin pulled taut across his cheekbones. He watched her with such intensity, she ought to have caught fire.

She *was* on fire. The pressure between her legs burned, but he shifted his touch and caressed her, using her own moisture to lubricate his penetration, enticing her to chase that capricious flutter that promised such exquisite pleasure.

He was saying things in Sicilian. Dirty things, maybe, but his tone was filled with praise and encouragement. Earthy pleasure. He didn't seem to care that she was being tentative. He groaned in suffering, but the fingers that dug into her hips didn't force her to take any more of him than she was ready for.

His intrusion hurt, but the internal stretch seemed to amplify her growing arousal. He kept caressing her, soothing her taut flesh with gentle fingers where they joined, then heightening her desire with circling touches across the straining button he'd anointed so mercilessly with his tongue.

She could hear herself making noises that bordered on distress as she hovered in the space between acute pain and profound pleasure. Such exquisite torture. How did anyone stand it?

"Give me your nipple," he coaxed in a voice that resonated from deep in his chest.

She did, leaning her breast closer to his mouth. The movement caused him to shift inside her, alarming her with the stinging sensation. She gasped, but as he suckled, she grew wetter and found herself sinking and lifting, seeking that hot friction. She was afraid to take all of him, but oh, it felt lovely to have the tip of him moving inside her.

This was the mysterious primeval knowledge she'd sought. This was the ethereal world she had heard existed between the poetic descriptions of sensual magnificence and the corporeal reality of sex. She had never understood how another's touch could be more gratifying than her own, but his hand and mouth and penetration became her entire world.

This man, with his head dropping back to watch her, somehow heightened everything about this experience into something exalted. His scent permeated the air she breathed and his lips tasted of her own essence. She sank all the way down, taking him fully inside her, and dazzlement turned his eyes silver. She could feel their sweat mingling, and their noises of pleasure were a perfect harmony.

She had never felt so connected to anyone. As they moved like this, they were essentially one being, experiencing together something that could not have happened apart. Not with anyone else, ever, anywhere. Only them. Here. Now. Like this.

As she rode up and down every last inch

of him, her arousal contracted to a tight point inside her. She stilled, fighting to hold back from the paradise she longed for, hovering on the brink of losing control.

"Giovanni," she breathed. "I'm—"

"Do it," he growled.

She moved with unfettered greed, thrilling at the feel of him buried deep inside her, and the euphoria of climax crept up on her. In a mindless need to have him with her, she scraped her thumb across his nipple and sucked his earlobe while her orgasm engulfed her, flooding her with shuddering ecstasy.

He locked his hands on her hips and his whole body clenched right before he released a ragged cry of gratification.

CHAPTER THREE

"MISSION ACCOMPLISHED," FREJA murmured next to him, pulling Giovanni from his post-coital doze.

He didn't want to come back to full consciousness. He would have to start picking apart exactly how unwise this had been, from the dinner he'd been urged to cancel to...*this*.

He shouldn't be feeling this smug when she had so completely destroyed him, leaving him more sated than any sexual experience he'd ever had.

Still, her odd choice of words penetrated his haze.

"Mission?" His voice had to be dug out of the depths of his chest and barely arrived above a graveled whisper. He turned his head on the pillow.

A decadent smile touched her lips. "I don't want to leave this bed."

He didn't want her to leave it, either. Ever. Realizing that was one of those moments when his life went out of focus and came back with finer edges and starker contrasts. It was sobering because he couldn't pretend things hadn't changed. *He* had.

"Not even to eat? I'm starving." He kept his tone light so he wouldn't betray how deeply affected he was. "I'll make a call, order in. Stay here." He had to make more than one call, but food was a good excuse to gain some distance and perspective. He sat up on the edge of the bed.

"I might shower if you don't mind?"

He looked over his shoulder. "Run a bath. I'll join you."

"Do you remember where my bag went?"

"*Bidduzza*, I'm having trouble remembering my own name."

She chuckled throatily and rose to hug him from behind. The cool swells of her breasts were against his back and her bent knees bracketed his hips. Her arms slithered around his neck and she gave his earlobe a light nip.

"Ouch." He protectively pinched it. Definitely a bath and a tutorial on his most sensitive erogenous zones. Sucking? Great. Biting? Not so much.

Which implied they would be doing this again.

Since when did he have such weak self-discipline?

"Sorry." Her soft breath wafted against his nape while her hair fell across his naked shoulder in a sensuous tickle. "I'm trying to thank you. That was wondrous."

"It was." Recognizing that, admitting it, increased his growing caution. He was very good at compartmentalizing, but needed to catch up on the filing. "I'll find your bag."

"I can." She rose and picked up his shirt, shook it out and pushed her arms into the sleeves. "Do you mind?" she asked with a glance as she did.

How could he? Not only was she a splendid picture of debauchery, rosy curves and shad-owed nipples visible beneath the fine linen, he experienced a Neanderthal-like thrill at seeing her in a garment that belonged to him. Not that he was such a throwback as to see *her* as a belonging, but he was aware of some-thing inside him locking into place. The kind of possessiveness that came of discovering something priceless and resolving to shelter it close. Protect and cherish.

Damn, that was unsettling. He had sexual

affairs, but always kept them as simple and casual as possible, yet here he felt the tug to follow when she moved out of sight into the bathroom. The water started running.

He pulled on his briefs and settled in his chair, picked up his pants, but his phone wasn't in them. On the table by the front door, perhaps.

"What do you feel like?" he asked when he found his phone and she joined him in the lounge. "There's a Thai place that's quite good." He thumbed through his contacts. "The vegan place is better, but it takes longer."

"You're vegan?"

"I have teams of people dedicated to my physical health. I eat what they make me. I should check the refrigerator. There's probably something there."

"Whatever you want is fine." She picked up her bag from the table and started to dig through it. "But I need lip balm before I eat. My lips feel like they're starting to chap. How do you think that happened?" She tucked her chin and elevated her brows in a scold.

"I have no idea. Let me kiss it better," he offered.

"Nice try. Not until—" She frowned. "Someone has been through my bag."

A guarded shiver chased over him, making him wish he'd put on more clothes. This was what came of letting sex make him complacent.

"Is something missing?" he asked with a suitable level of concern, even though he was damned confident nothing would be. "I can't imagine anyone at the restaurant went into it, but I can make a call."

She set the bag back on the table while she took a thorough inventory. "Everything seems to be here." She counted some bills, rearranged the order of them before she folded them back into a pocket.

"How do you know someone's been through it?" Only spies like him tended to set up little traps to betray those who might enter where they weren't invited.

"I've lived out of a suitcase most of my life. I arrange all my bags so I can get what I want without looking and can always tell when a maid or customs agent has rummaged through. I *never* put my lip balm in that pocket." She tsked. "Maybe tell the restaurant to be on the lookout for pickpockets?"

"I'll call them after I order the food. Join you in a minute," he promised.

She disappeared and he tapped to call Everett.

"You left early," was Everett's abrupt greeting. Perhaps that was the reason his minion had been so sloppy in the search of Freja's bag.

"Anything?" Giovanni asked.

"Two passports. American and Swedish."

That fact had been in the dossier Everett had provided on Giovanni's request, the one that had included her extensive debriefing after her two-year stint in a North Korean village, the names of her contacts at university, and the particulars of her book deal. The general consensus among government agencies was that she *could* be a foreign operative, but no one had been able to prove it or determine who employed her.

"That's it?" Giovanni prompted.

"She was prepared to spend the night with you." Everett's tone held a warning.

Giovanni dismissed her changes of clothes with a meaningless grunt. Freja had been coming from work. Plenty of women were veritable tortoises, carrying their entire boudoir everywhere they went.

"I have a car waiting to take her home," Everett said.

"Unnecessary." Giovanni didn't even pause to think about it.

A potent silence on the other end told him he ought to.

"Do you mind if I have dessert?" Freja asked, jolting him with her sudden reappearance. "I have a hideous sweet tooth. Chocolate?"

"Done," he assured her, saying to Everett, "Did you get that? Add dessert to my order. Something with chocolate. Leave it with the doorman."

"Do you know what you're doing?"

"Absolutely," Giovanni lied dismissively. "Good night."

The massive triangular jetted tub was set into a corner of the palatial master bath. The tiled edges were set at a height that made it easy for Giovanni to transfer back and forth from his chair. The windows fogged from the steam off the water, but otherwise offered a clear view of the city.

"I'll have to tell the doorman he can eat the Thai delivery," Giovanni said as they finished what his Sicilian nutritionist had left in the refrigerator.

He hadn't bothered to heat the chickpea

fritters or saffron risotto balls. They'd gobbled them down cold with antipasto and scoops of savory pistachio sauce. He'd even brought a handful of chocolate chip cookies from the freezer. They tasted amazing with the rich red wine they were sipping from stemless glasses.

As he reached to set the tray on the floor beside the edge of the tub, the jets went off. She realized he'd put on music when he'd lowered the lights. Feathery strokes of guitar played over the soothing breaths and lazy keys of an accordion.

He settled back with a sigh of repletion and invited, "Come here."

She shyly drifted from her seat opposite and he drew her in front of him. She reclined upon him, head pillowed by his shoulder as he stretched his long arms along the tub's edge and absently adjusted the handheld spray washer in its holder.

"What if we fall asleep like this?" she asked, eyelids heavy.

"Then we will wake up very cold and wrinkly."

She smiled and they were quiet for a few minutes.

"Will you tell me about your time in North Korea?" he asked.

Her defenses were so low, she felt thin and fragile as his question penetrated. Hot emotion rushed into her eyes and she turned her face against his bicep in an instinctive flinch.

"Can't you just read it?" Telling him the story, when she was this defenseless, felt too hard.

"You don't want to tell me?" Subtle tension hardened the body that cradled hers.

"It makes me sad. And no one will let me *be* sad. They want me to be angry. And grateful that I was rescued."

"Aren't you?"

"I'm grateful to be in a country where I can talk and move freely, obviously. But I'm equally grateful to have had a home there. I wasn't as miserable there as people want me to be."

"You said your father's editor didn't send him there. What were you two doing there? Why did he drag you into the farthest reaches of China, never mind North Korea?"

"That was his job," she defended her father for what felt like the millionth time. It amazed her how many people criticized him for taking his daughter into remote parts of the world when his tales of parenting while trying to avoid yellow fever, Zika, and old-fashioned travel tummy were the reasons for his great appeal. "Taking impulsive side trips was very normal for us. We were visiting the crater lake in the nature preserve on the border between China and North Korea when the opportunity came up to join a tour to see the other side. Pappa was always trying to make a point that people are just people and that nearly every place in the world is safe to visit if you're respectful. It was, but we were hiking in the foothills of the mountains when he had the stroke. The guide had to run to ask villagers to come back with a vehicle to carry him down. He had passed by the time they got us to the clinic."

"I'm so sorry." His voice was a grave, reassuring rumble against her back. His arm slid under the water and around her waist, holding her comfortingly close. "That must have been terrifying. You were seventeen?"

"Yes. And the rest of our tour had to move on. Our guide left me at the clinic with my father's body. I saw the guide hand my passport to an official in a military uniform. I thought, *That's bad*, but there wasn't anything I could do."

"Could you speak the language at all?"

"Only rudimentary words like 'please' and 'thank you.' Byung-woo was the doctor who wrote out Pappa's death certificate. He and his wife, Sung-mi, lived upstairs. I was a wreck, obviously. She brought me a cup of tea and I could see her pretending not to listen to the men. She was being very stoic, but I could tell whatever they were saying was bad. I did the only thing I could think of. I tried to hand all my money to Sung-mi."

"Bribery," he said with disdain. "That quaint and reliable solution to any problem."

"I pretended I was trying to finance a proper burial for my father."

"And?"

"She took it into the room where the men were talking and they closed the door. A little while later, the official left and Sung-mi and Byung-woo brought my father's body into a special room and helped me lay him out. Villagers came by over the next few days, sat with me while I grieved. Then they took him back into the mountains and we buried him in a small graveyard."

"So he's still there."

"Yes." And she thought it somewhat appropriate that he rested as he had lived, an interloper accepted in a land that wasn't his own.

"Did you try to leave at that point?"

"Foreigners aren't allowed to use public transport. There was no internet. Things like booking a flight or online banking… All those things people take for granted weren't available to me. My cash was gone. The few times Pappa and I had talked about what I should do if he passed, Pappa always said that Oliver would help me settle his affairs, so I went to that same official. I gave him a letter to mail for me. Open, of course. I made sure it said how well I was being treated and that I only wished to leave because I felt I was a burden on my hosts—which I was."

"He mailed it? You said earlier that the Swedish government was the first to get involved."

"Oliver never got the letter, but the guide made a report about my father's death. More officials turned up. That's when I realized I was being officially detained, but I guess my letter reassured them. They left me in the custody of Byung-woo and Sung-mi instead of sending me to a work camp or jail."

"Why would they risk taking in a stranger? One from the West no less?"

That cool, inquisitive tone of his bothered her. She started to sit up, but his arm stayed heavy across her waist. After a disgruntled moment, she sank back into him.

"When Sung-mi brought me upstairs that first night, she put me in a tiny room under the slant of the roof. It had a single bed with a handmade quilt. There was a chair with a doll in it and a pair of child's glasses on the table. There was a box of puzzles beneath the bed."

"Ah," he said with solemn understanding.

"Yes. Their daughter was sick her whole life and died when she was twelve. Sung-mi talked about her a lot. That's how I learned Korean. She taught me to cook and took me to the sewing circles where the local women made uniforms for the army. In many ways, she became the mother I'd missed all my life. Byung-woo was kind, too. He took me fishing sometimes. We barely spoke, but we sat by the river for hours."

"Sounds idyllic."

"Not really." Her wandering gaze landed on the square head of the handheld shower nozzle. She realized it perfectly reflected his face in its gold surface.

"No? Why not?" His voice lazily encouraged her to confide, but she jolted as she realized he was looking right at her in that tiny reflection.

He casually turned his head so his mouth nuzzled into her hair.

"I, um…"

She didn't know what disconcerted her more, the realization he might have been watching her the whole time she'd been talking or his languid return to assaulting her senses. Beneath the water, he cupped her breast and gently massaged.

"What were you saying?" He nibbled along her nape.

"Hmm? Oh. That I had to be very careful," she recalled dimly, tilting her head to expose more of her neck. "We were under constant surveillance." Her nipple tightened to stab into his palm. "My classmates at university didn't understand how I cared for my hosts and wanted to protect them as much as myself. They said that sort of thing makes me a traitor."

"Are you?"

"No." She twisted to face him.

His eyelids were heavy, but his gaze keen beneath. All he said was, "Good." And he pressed his mouth to hers. They didn't talk again until he said, "We should take this to the bed."

* * *

Giovanni had been fifteen when the car his father had been driving was broadsided and sent over an embankment, rolling three times before coming to rest. Everyone else had been killed instantly. Giovanni had spent a year in hospital, enduring endless pain and surgeries that culminated in amputation of his remaining leg when a stubborn infection had forced him to choose between his limb or his life.

He'd always been stubborn and competitive, but it had taken two more years of grit and effort before he felt comfortable in this new body, learning how it worked and ultimately achieving the independence he craved.

He'd never stopped hitting on girls. Charm was a quality Sicilian men possessed by law. He'd become sexually active around the same time as his peers, but there'd been a steeper learning curve for him when it came to giving and receiving pleasure.

Until a few days ago, he'd been satisfied with the frequency and quality of lovemaking he engaged in and thought he had it all figured out.

Freja was rewriting his entire scope of experience.

He kept telling himself he was only continuing to see her for investigative purposes, but as day four dawned and they'd barely been out of each other's sight since dinner that first night, he had to admit it was the sex. He couldn't keep his hands off her.

He had tried to take her home. Their first lazy morning had turned into an indolent afternoon, but she'd been scheduled to work that evening. His driver had parked outside her building and their goodbye in the back seat of his town car had turned into a steamy suggestion that she call in sick.

She'd left him long enough to run up to her flat for her laptop and to pack a small bag. She'd been here ever since, coaching a couple of her Korean students over video chat, helping with their English pronunciation and offering feedback on some writing assignments. She had made no effort to hide any of it while Giovanni answered emails on the other side of the room.

Yesterday, they'd strolled through the park, but the rest of the days they had stayed in. They worked, ate, swam, and waited for his small army of aids, therapists, assistants and housekeepers to leave so they could make love and lounge around half-dressed.

They had intimate encounters constantly.

A light kiss turned into heavy petting that turned into an intense, inventive interlude. Other times he woke from a lengthy debauched session that had left him wrung out and supremely satisfied. His sense of contentment lingered into those moments when he turned his head to find her beside him, blinking awake and smiling through a yawn.

Those unguarded moments were the best and the worst. They convinced him she was exactly as she seemed—unusual, but ultimately harmless. For a woman who hadn't had a lover until a few days ago, however, she was taking to it like a duck to water. That forced him to ask himself if he was being played by a champion manipulator.

Even Everett was starting to worry, sounding impatient when Giovanni accepted his call. "She's still there. *Why?*"

Giovanni bit back asking Everett if he'd ever gotten laid, because he definitely should try it sometime.

"I'm in the pool." Despite the April rain spitting from the overcast sky. "What do you need?"

"Leave early and plan for a week in France in June," Everett said in crisp tone.

Giovanni didn't ask why. Everett would

have a contact he wanted Giovanni to intercept or a party he wanted him to observe. It was the work he'd signed on for, but as he watched Freja continue to lap the pool in a graceful crawl, Giovanni resented Everett's claim on his time. He wasn't ready for this liaison to end.

Which was the most compelling reason it should.

"Sure," he muttered and clicked off his phone, sliding it into the pocket of his robe where it hung next to his pool lift. He pushed away from the ledge and windmilled a backstroke until he crossed paths with Freja.

She stopped to catch her breath. They both hooked an arm on the ledge.

"Is everything okay?" She pushed her wet hair off her face. "You look annoyed."

"Details about my trip. I'm leaving early." He had deliberately mentioned this trip their first evening. He was always clear with women that he wasn't looking for anything but a brief, enjoyable dalliance.

That same evening, Freja had called him a sexist for suggesting she aspired to marry and have children. Inexperienced she might be, but she wasn't immature. There were no unrealistic fantasies dancing in her eyes. There was no guilt trip that he had been leading her on. She expressed exactly the right pout of disappointment, then turned it into a rueful smile.

"Probably for the best." She wrinkled her nose. "The owner of the catering company asked if I should be admitted to hospital, I've called in sick so many times."

He slid his free arm around her waist, floating her into contact with his chest. Swimming always aroused him, but the desire sizzling in his wiring was all for her. That and the tendrils of possessiveness that were becoming barbed hooks within him as their time together drew to a close.

It was a potent combination that charged what was supposed to be a leisurely kiss into one with more ferocious greed than he intended.

She stiffened in surprise, then melted into him, greeting his tongue with her own as she moaned and coiled her limbs around him.

This was why he still had her here after four days. This response of hers was addictive.

He flexed his arm on the ledge to secure them at the edge of the pool and slid his other hand into the bottom of her suit, palming her bare ass. He'd had time to learn what she liked, and that always made her squirm. She tightened her thighs around his waist and rocked her hips against him.

She knew his triggers, too. She swooped her lips across to suck his earlobe until he could hardly keep their heads above water.

The strings on her bikini were too much bother. He caught the neck strap and stretched it to bring it up and forward, dropping it away under the water between them. Her pale breasts with their pink tips sat just below the surface, pretty and tempting.

He scooped his arm under her butt and lifted her enough that he could suck her nipples, each one going cold and hard as a pebble in the brisk spring air.

"Giovanni," she gasped, hands scraping through his hair and roaming restlessly over his shoulders. "Let's go to the bedroom."

"So impatient," he teased grittily, even though that eagerness of hers never ceased to thrill him. Hell, he was right there with her, feeling so damned ravenous he didn't want to let her go for the time it would take to dry off and get to the bed. How would he go months without her when he couldn't bear to wait five minutes?

"I want to feel all of you," she said with a pang in her voice and a drift of her touch to delicately pinch his nipple.

He shuddered in reaction, nearly losing his grip on the ledge.

She chuckled softly as she dropped back into the water with a slosh. They were nose to nose again, mouth fusing to mouth with insatiate need. He shoved his hand in her bottoms again, squeezing her cheek and sliding his touch under her thigh. There. His long fingers reached the plump folds and fine hairs. A sweet noise throbbed in her throat as he found the heart of her response.

"If you want all of me, take me," he said against her mouth. Distant warning bells sounded in his head, but he ignored them. "I want to feel you, too." He deepened his touch, shaking with want at the idea of being naked inside her.

"H-here?" She blinked dazed eyes at him. "Without a condom?"

He wore them to protect his health. "I don't ejaculate," he reminded her.

Her hand dropped into the space between them. She pushed the front of his bathing suit down, freeing his erection. The cool of the water did nothing to chill his ardor. He pulled aside the crotch of her bathing suit, his thumb lingering to coax another jagged noise out of her.

She guided the head of his erection against her folds. Slowly he was enfolded in heat, a sensation so acute his whole body felt as though he was thrust into a furnace.

His one rational thought was that he shouldn't let them drown, but— He tilted his head back and swore his gratification at the overcast, spitting sky. "You're so *hot*."

"You feel good, too," she gasped, curling her arms and legs around him, clinging as they kissed and kissed.

The suspension of the water gave him more ability to thrust than he usually had. He used his arm to cushion her against the hard, tiled wall, but gripping the ledge, he was able to use his whole body to make love to her. It was incredibly exciting. The water swirled around them, further stimulating him, while Freja moved in response, making those gorgeous noises that told him he was giving her great pleasure.

He wanted to slow down and make this last forever, it was so impossibly good, but the intensity was more than he could control.

"Giovanni," she gasped in the fractured breath of approaching climax.

"Come," he coaxed, speaking Sicilian because his own crisis gathered like a condensed ball of energy, ready to explode. "It's too good. I can't hold back."

He didn't want to. Ecstasy beckoned.

As the last of his discipline shredded, she released a cry of elation and convulsed against him. A ragged, "Freja," tore from his throat as his entire body shuddered in a way he hadn't experienced in years.

CHAPTER FOUR

FREJA WAS FEELING very subdued as she and Giovanni showered off the salt from the pool.

The shower was enormous with a dozen heads and nozzles and taps. He had a special chair he used in here, but there was still plenty of room for her. He'd even had his housekeeper purchase some organic, vanilla-scented body wash and shampoo, making it super easy to linger in the warm spray.

Or maybe she was seizing the excuse to draw out her last few minutes with him. Once she dried off and dressed, she would have to say goodbye and she didn't feel ready.

Not that she could say so. Giovanni was a sophisticated man. This was the sort of transitory affair that consenting adults engaged in. She kept reminding herself that this was a rite of passage on her part. It was her first tumble into physical intimacy, one that was paired with deep infatuation with a dynamic man. Getting her heart bruised was all part of the process.

If anything, she ought to view the termination of their affair as a healthy end point. They were ending things in a civilized and, frankly, necessary way. In recent years, she'd grown used to being autonomous and making her own decisions, but these last few days, she had found herself accommodating his presence in her life, trying to maximize the limited time she had with him. That was fine for a weekend, but arranging her world around a man had its pitfalls. She knew that.

Nevertheless, the sense of abandonment that engulfed her as their goodbye loomed threatened to crush her.

"You're being very quiet," Giovanni noted, turning off the sprayer he was using.

"Hmm? Oh." She tilted back her head to give her hair one last unneeded rinse, not wanting him to see the morose expression on her face. Her worst nightmare was to behave like some gauche teenager at the last minute. "I'm thinking of all those very compelling things like whether I need to pick up milk on my way home."

She turned off her showerhead and accepted the towel he handed her. She stayed in the shower to dry off while he rolled out to the spot under the heat lamp.

She realized he was being very quiet as well, sitting up straighter to saw the towel across his back, but watching her closely. Anxious for her to leave? She wrapped the towel around herself and stepped out with a meaningless smile plastered on her face.

"Freja." He reached out as she came even with him and tugged the bottom corner of her towel.

She scrabbled to secure it, letting out a laugh only to sober when she realized he wasn't trying to playfully steal it, only to get her attention. The gravity in his expression made her heart lurch.

"What's wrong?" Her hand instinctively tightened on the towel.

"Do you realize that I may have made you pregnant just now?"

"What?" She stumbled back a few steps, bumping into the edge of the sink.

"Are you going to faint?" He pushed forward and set a hard hand at her hip.

She kept one hand clenched in the towel, the other gripped the sink. "But you said—"

"I know." He gave a slight shrug that only

hinted at sheepish because she didn't see a lot of embarrassment or remorse in him. "It was the last thing I expected and I could be wrong. The way it felt in the pool, though... I can't explain it, but it was different. I'm pretty sure I came inside you."

"But..." Maybe she was going to faint because her gaze couldn't seem to land on a stationary spot in the room and everything seemed to be spinning. "What should I do?"

"Come here." He nudged even closer and drew her into his lap.

She kind of collapsed, joints not wanting to support her.

He caught her, of course. She'd watched him do pull-ups while strapped into his workout chair, lifting the combined weight with what looked like effortless ease. His upper body was insanely strong, his arms the most secure place she could ever be.

"I feel so stupid," she mumbled. "The one thing I didn't want was for you to think I was naive just because I've never done this before. Unprotected sex is *such* a rookie move."

"Tell me about it. I know better myself."

She met his gaze hoping for humor, but the austere lines in his face dug into her heart like a shard of broken glass.

"I guess I take one of those morning-after pills?"

He didn't answer right away and she didn't look at him. She didn't realize she was chewing her thumbnail until he took her hand and eased it into her lap.

"It's possible nothing will happen. Paraplegic men have all sorts of fertility issues. Low counts…"

"Do you?"

"I have no idea what my count is. I've never been tested for it. Having children was always something I shelved in the back of my mental cupboard. I didn't imagine I could reach it without medical intervention." His thumb was wearing a restless circle into the back of her hand. "Obviously, it's your body, your choice, but I would like to wait and see what happens."

"What?" If he hadn't been holding her so firmly in his lap, she would have tumbled out and onto the floor in a splat of shock.

"I'm asking you not to take any pills. The chance you'll conceive is really low, but…" Huskiness crept into his tone. "I'd like to take that chance."

"Just…wait?" She couldn't make sense of any of it. That this was a thing that could happen, that he wanted her to *let* it happen. "But you're leaving," she reminded him, as if she needed him around to "wait and see." His part in such things was over.

"Well, you'll have to come to Europe with me," he stated as though that was obvious.

"I can't go to *Europe* with you!" Now she did find her legs and stood on both of them.

She realized he was still naked in his chair and entirely too confident and powerful in his natural state. He sent a circumspect look up at her.

"Why not? If it's a passport issue, I have people who can sort that very quickly."

"My passport is fine." She was pathological about keeping both of hers current. "But I have a job. Bills."

"It's catering." He dismissed it with a flick of his fingers. "They'll give your shifts to the next person on the list."

"And skip me in future because I'm unreliable. They'll fire me outright if they find out I'm seeing you. We're not supposed to fraternize with guests."

"That's not even an argument." He went through to the adjacent closet and found a pair of blue boxers, staying where he could see her as he pulled them on. "Catering is hardly a career you love or planned to do forever."

"I still need it. I have a flat to pay for."

"Lease it."

"Oh, just like that," she scoffed. "I'm not going to hand my keys to the first stranger who answers an ad. It takes time to find someone suitable."

"It takes a phone call to my property agent. She'll have someone with impeccable references in it tomorrow. And before you bring up your blogging or tutoring work, you've done both from this apartment. You can do them from anywhere with a Wi-Fi connection."

"Wow. Must be nice to solve all your problems with your bank account."

"It is," he assured her as she came into the closet, where he had pulled on a shirt and was working on his pants.

She found her own underwear in the drawer his housekeeper had allotted her. "Well, excuse me for pointing out the obvious, but my blog and tutoring income won't cover first-class airfare, let alone support me at your standard of living." The monthly cost of heating his rooftop pool was probably more than her mortgage payment. "I can't afford the type of hotels you stay in, either. Don't say you'll pay my way," she warned with a pointed finger.

"I travel by private jet," he said pithily. "One more body on board is a name on a manifest, no extra expense. Same goes for the hotels. Much of my stay will be in properties I own. I prefer spaces equipped to suit my needs. Feel free to cook if you're worried about the cost of food. I'm not."

She stood there feeling impotent, damp hair causing runnels of water to tickle irritatingly down her back. "I can't just—"

"Why not?" he cut in with a lift of his arrogant brows.

"Frankly?" She gave her wet hair a flick. "After spending most of my life following a man around the world, I'm not that keen to do it again."

She stepped into a pair of jeans and a light pullover, then looked for her empty suitcase to pack it.

"I've reached the part in your book where your father had the stroke," he said quietly. "It's difficult to read. Your writing is beautiful. Poignant. But it put a knife in my stomach that is twisted by every word. I had to stop."

She dropped her hands to her sides. He was the most disarming man!

"Thank you?" she mumbled, eyes burning white-hot.

"I keep thinking about that tour you're expected to do. I don't want to see your heartache exploited for book sales. Are you sure you want that?"

"No. But it's different when it's strangers. I don't care what they think." She hugged herself and gave him a disgruntled side-eye. "I worry what you think, though."

His stormy gray gaze was too intense to hold. "Why? Do you have something to hide?"

"No."

He left an expectant silence for her to fill, but she didn't know what he wanted her to say. Her heart panged with unexpected and acute inadequacy. And yearning. He was even more of a mystery to her than she was to him.

This was the crux of her worry about his effect on her, she realized. He touched her as though she was delicate china, brought her to the heights of pleasure and gave her free rein to explore his body. He let her sleep in his bed and share his bath and gave her his Wi-Fi password, but there was an invisible wall between them. He kept himself deeply guarded and impenetrable, but expected her to somehow reveal her whole self to him.

When she didn't say anything, he rolled close and encircled her wrist with his loose grip. "You said you were struggling for blog content. Wouldn't traveling help?"

"I could take a trip on my own if I thought that was the answer."

"Would you please quit arguing?" His eyes turned pewter with molten emotions. "If you're pregnant with my child, I want to look after you both."

And there went her knees turning to gelatin again.

"What happens if I am? We've known each other *four days*, Giovanni."

"Then things will accelerate even more."

Her choked laugh was more a sob of helplessness.

"Many couples have unprotected sex for years and don't conceive." The stiff defensiveness in him cut through better than anything else might have. "This is very much a long shot, Freja."

"It's not that I don't *want* your baby, Giovanni. Only that I'm still figuring out my own life. It makes it hard to imagine being responsible for someone else's, especially one so vulnerable."

"You won't be doing that alone. That's why I want you to come with me."

She shook her head, unable to believe she was doing this, but she knew she would regret it if she didn't take this chance to spend a little more time with him, to see if it could turn into more.

"Okay," she agreed.

Pregnant?

It shouldn't be such a shocking possibility for a woman who was having regular sex, but Freja was completely unprepared for the idea. She fell inward as she processed it, existing in a sort of meditative state, barely participating in the real world beyond the necessary preparations for travel with Giovanni. She quit her catering job and advised her students their schedule would be changing. She leased her apartment and put a few things in storage.

Giovanni told her not to pack more than one case, which was hilarious because she always traveled light, but he added, "My people will ensure you have everything you need."

Even her father hadn't been that arrogant. He'd paid her for odd jobs and photos, then sent her along to the local shops to find her own feminine products and shoes that fit. She had saved up for her own laptop as a teenager, rather than using her father's castoff, but that was as materialistic as she got.

So relying on Giovanni and letting his schedule dictate hers felt both natural and challenging. When she tried to imagine adding another body and personality to the equation, her brain shorted out and wandered down impractical paths of potential baby names instead.

Not that she could resent Giovanni for turning her life upside down. He might be formidable, but he was also remarkable. He commanded respect not just for his wealth or the confidence that carried him along so well, but for the person he was beneath.

He might not reveal much about himself, but she was catching glimpses. He made dry remarks that had his physical therapist snickering and came up with fresh solutions over conference calls with his development teams. He even generously shoehorned a last-minute charity event into his packed schedule.

"You're on board with that?" she dimly heard him ask. His voice firmed. "Freja?"

"Hmm? Sorry, I thought you were talking

to someone else." She was barely tracking what was going on in his stylish, contemporary villa on the outskirts of Milan. She'd slept on the plane, so she'd been awake half the night. Now the stylist was turning her in circles, taking her measurements while someone else made notes. Another assistant flashed swatches while yet another was in a huddle with the young man who seemed to be charged with organizing Giovanni's calendar. She kept hearing color-related questions like, "Red carpet? Black tie or white?"

"*Ciau.* Welcome back to the conversation," Giovanni teased as she blinked at him. "I know I said we would use today to recover from jet lag and get your wardrobe started, but I'm accepting an invitation for this evening. It's a good cause. A sport program for child amputees."

"Oh. Yes, I heard you say that. So you're going out tonight? Of course. Do whatever you normally would. I'll probably be asleep before dinner."

"*We* are going out," he said dryly. "But you can nap this afternoon if you need to. Can you have something ready by then?" He directed that to the stylist.

"Of course. Shall I book one of my technicians to help with hair and makeup?"

"Thank you."

Freja would have argued that she was capable of putting on her own lipstick, but someone else came in with a call for him and they weren't alone again until several hours later. By then, they'd flown to Monaco.

The flight was less than an hour, but it added to her sense of disorientation. They were given a penthouse in the hotel. It was very swanky and staff were buzzing around, shifting furniture and taking orders.

Giovanni caught her stifling a yawn, and said, "Go lie down. I'll join you as soon as I finish my calls. The desk will wake us when your dress arrives."

That was indeed what happened, tying her up for another hour. By the time she joined him in the lounge, she was more scattered and overwhelmed than ever.

His head went back and he raked his gaze down the one-shouldered dress in a color the stylist had called "Egyptian blue."

"I thought you were beautiful in a catering uniform that did you no favors. This…" His attention came back to her face and his brows snapped together. "Are you unwell? If this was too much for you, you should have said."

"It is too much, but not in the way you mean. This is an *evening* gown, Giovanni!" She plucked at the beaded silk, accidentally opening the slit that climbed to midthigh.

"Call me old-fashioned, but when I'm on a date, I prefer to be the one wearing the tuxedo."

And he looked amazing in his dove-white jacket over a white shirt and scrupulously tailored black pants. His bow tie was black, as was his satin pocket square.

"Is the dress not comfortable? You look fantastic." His appreciative gaze took a second, slower tour down to her silver gladiator heels. "I'm regretting that we're already late because I would love to see you in *just* those." His gaze lingered on her shoes.

"What about these?" She gave the earrings dangling off her lobes an askance bobble. They were exquisite cascades of blue sapphires and white diamonds, and had to be worth a small country's GDP.

"Those, too," he said throatily. "Now I'll be hard all evening, picturing you in only those earrings and those shoes. Thanks."

"That's not—" She almost stamped her foot. "The stylist told me they're *real*."

"As opposed to imaginary?"

"As opposed to costume. When you said we were attending a casino fundraiser, I thought that meant a casino *theme*. That we would go to a bingo hall or the back of a pub where you wager with vouchers and bid on prizes like movie tickets in a bucket of flavored popcorn." That was the sort of fundraiser she'd attended at university.

"Ah. No. Real casino, real money."

She suspected he was laughing at her as he moved to press the button for their private elevator. It was small, so she let him back his chair in before she joined him.

"I'll stake you fifty thousand euros, though," he added.

"I'm not going to gamble your money!"

"You don't like gambling? No worries. There's a silent auction. I'll stake you fifty thousand for that, too."

"I'm not going to throw your money away on silly prizes, either!"

"Should I just write the check and we'll stay in the room?" His tone cooled. "It's a very reputable organization, Freja. They're getting my money either way. I thought we'd enjoy a proper date and let them have the scoop on announcing our relationship, to get them extra exposure. I'd rather we were old news by the time I finalize my acquisition of the airline later this week."

The elevator stopped and she rocked on her heels, realizing she had underestimated him in the most bizarre way. She had known he was rich, but it hadn't penetrated that he was "acquire an airline" rich.

The doors opened and she made an effort to rearrange her flabbergasted expression, but how was she supposed to process any of this?

He lifted a brow, waiting for her to make up her mind.

"Are you calling our first date *im*proper?" she finally asked.

The corner of his mouth twitched. He scratched his upper lip and said, "One could argue either way, I think."

He waved for her to precede him out of the elevator.

It was a short walk through the mild evening from the hotel into the casino. The lavishness of their hotel suite hadn't prepared her for the opulence of the casino. She tried not to gawk as they were shown through a massive hall where a stained-glass dome dominated the ceiling. Ornate gold filigree framed what had to be hand-painted frescoes, and crystal chandeliers sparkled over the various gaming tables.

She had barely caught a glimpse of the spinning images on the slot machines before they were shown through a passageway between marble columns, into a private salon.

If she had thought the main hall a monument to luxury, here was where indulgence met taste in all forms. The clatter of tourists and seasoned gamblers was shut out by a small orchestra providing a refined background to the smooth conversation and cultivated laughter. Men and women in stunning evening wear milled around gaming tables and hovered near the bar, all casually flashing jewels and gold watches, tiaras and even a ceremonial sword hanging off the hip of a decorated military officer.

"Giovanni!" A lovely blonde with a soft British accent greeted him warmly, bending to kiss each of his cheeks. "You're too good to us, flying in at the last minute like this. Hello. I'm Clair. Thank you for coming." The woman offered to shake Freja's hand.

"Freja Anderson, Clair Dmitriev. Clair is on the board of several charities that benefit children, this one included," Giovanni explained. He asked after Clair's children and husband.

"Oh, everyone has teeth either coming in or falling out, but otherwise we're all well."

"Aleksy, too?" he asked dryly, making her chuckle with enjoyment.

"Not unless he's losing his gold fillings at the poker table." She glanced toward the back of the room. "I told him you were coming. He's looking forward to catching up with you. Don't you dare outbid him on the necklace in the auction. It's to die for," she told Freja with a sigh of admiration. "An amazing goldsmith out of Budapest donated it. I'm so sorry for rushing away. I have to straighten out a mix-up with the presentation, but I'll check in with you again as soon as I can."

"That's how she does it," Giovanni said with laconic amusement as Clair hurried away. "If she wanted the necklace that badly, her husband would have already bought it for her. But let's see if we can start a bidding war over it."

The necklace was beautiful and Giovanni doubled the current bid, earning a frosty look from a woman in a sea-green gown. He offered a small fortune for a rare bottle of cognac and another for a hand-blown vase.

"Ah. You need luggage," he said as they paused before the designer set.

It had a vintage carpetbag look trimmed in brown leather with gold clasps and hinges. The ensemble included four suitcases of various sizes, a steamer trunk, a shoe chest, a jewelry case, a garment bag and a hatbox. It claimed to have a value of eighty thousand euros.

Giovanni put a one in front of that figure.

"What are you doing?" she hissed, appalled.

"Winning."

"I need *a* suitcase." For underwear. "All the eveningwear is on loan, isn't it?"

He sent her a look that asked if she was missing several marbles. "This is why I find you endlessly fascinating. I can never tell if you're feeding me a line like you did about being married, or if you're actually that naive."

"Are you serious?" Her stomach dropped to the middle of the earth. "Please tell me these are loans." She pointed at her ears.

"I thought they would suit you and they do. This says they'll monogram each piece." He nodded at the bidding sheet. "That's a nice touch, don't you think?" He scratched off his bid and increased it, then rolled along, leaving her speechless.

She was still trying to come to terms with the idea she could, however unlikely, be pregnant. Now she began to understand what it would mean if she was. She would be part of Giovanni's life. Part of *this*. The high fashion and high rollers, the titled and the privileged.

Freja had spent her whole life as an odd duck. She had learned to embrace her status as an outsider and press forward on that left foot so she wouldn't be shunned completely. She didn't expect to be accepted into the different cultures she encountered, but it meant she'd spent most of her life feeling apart from everyone around her. She'd had her father for company and later Sung-mi, but even they had eventually fallen away. She had never found "my people, my home."

Then she'd come to America and encountered the strangest culture shock of all. In New York, everyone stuck out so no one did. She hadn't realized how comfortable she'd been there until she failed to blend in again.

She didn't belong here! This crowd drowned odd ducks in orange sauce and ate them with roasted beets.

She didn't even want to belong here. She had grown up on a shoestring, not living in poverty, but often a witness to it. She still lived very frugally, not liking to see waste when she knew how hard some people worked for the little they had.

"I'm going to try my luck at the craps table," Giovanni said.

She nodded. "I'm going to read the…" She gestured absently at the display of framed stories about children the charity had helped.

It was an excuse to steal a moment to catch her breath, but soon she was losing herself in each of the success stories. Children hurt by land mines or illness or pure bad luck were all finding purpose and achieving bigger things than ribbons and bronze medallions. They wore smiles and pride and confidence. Each photo lifted Freja's heart a little more until she was smiling to herself with happiness for them.

Darn him, this *was* a good cause. She couldn't be angry with him for being wretchedly generous in supporting it. She went to his side and set a hand on his shoulder.

"I'm losing. Give me some lady luck." He showed her the dice in his hand.

She blew on them and he threw.

A roar of approval went up around the table.

It was the beginning of a hot streak that had people betting in an increasing frenzy. She blew each time while Giovanni stacked up chips before him. She couldn't help holding her breath, then bursting with a cheer of laughter with everyone else when the sevens kept coming up. She was completely caught up in the play as the stakes rose higher and higher.

Suddenly Giovanni said, "That's a million." He pushed his stack of chips toward the stickman. "Donate it to the foundation."

There was another loud reaction from the spectators, this one a mix of shock and approval with a few moans that their luck was changing as someone else moved in to throw the dice.

Freja and Giovanni ran a small gauntlet of congratulations before settling into a quieter area of the room to sample the canapés and enjoy complimentary champagne sent over by Clair.

"Please don't ever put me through a roller coaster like that again. I don't think my heart can stand it." Freja set her hand on her chest, still breathless. "I thought you were here because you're a big softie who can't resist helping injured children, but you're actually an adrenaline junkie who enjoys risk, aren't you?"

"Aren't you?"

He might have meant it as light banter, but she heard the edge in his voice that invaded sometimes, the one that made her feel as though he saw something in her that wasn't there. The crash of his gaze into her own made her heart stutter and trip.

Every time she thought she was coming to know him a little, he had one of these mercurial shifts that disoriented her again. He did have a taste for risk. For one second, he let her see there was an atavistic barbarian in him willing to fight to the death if he had to.

She ought to have gone cold with premonition, but something in her leaped toward that Neanderthal the way a stray fleck of metal latched on to a magnet.

She was so shocked by her reaction, she yanked her gaze from his and tried to steady her breathing, but she was left teetering upon an intrinsic difference between them—as if they needed more proof beyond this enormous wealth gap.

"No," she said quietly but firmly. "Some people enjoy the tension of a haunted house, but I don't put myself in scary situations if I can avoid it. I've been genuinely frightened and I braved it out because I wanted to survive, but I don't like it. I'm here *in spite* of my fear."

"You're afraid right now? Why?" His steel gaze kept swooping into hers, catching like talons into her heart.

"It's obvious, isn't it? We're very different, but we might wind up tied to each other for life."

"I'm not frightened of that."

"Of course *you're* not!" She laughed, but there was mild hysteria in it.

He narrowed his eyes. "What does that mean?"

"It means it's one thing to lower into a cage and admire the shark. It's quite another to swim in the open water with him. I'm not a shark." She tapped her breastbone.

"You want me to believe you're a goldfish? I don't."

"And you want me to believe after that display—" she pointed in the direction of the craps table "—that you'll be happy stuck in a bowl with me and a guppy you didn't ask for. I don't."

"You don't know me," he bit out.

She choked on the irony of that while he sat back, mouth pinned flat with frustration.

After a moment, she sighed and leaned forward to set her hand on his sleeve.

"The fact that my experience is strange enough to write a book about it makes people think I'm a lot more interesting than I am. I don't actually want to be the most interesting person in the room. There's a lot more security in being exactly the same."

"Is that what you want? Security?" A muscle in his cheek ticked. "Because I can definitely give you that."

"Financial security is important." There was no denying that. "But I'm talking about emotional security." And neither was likely to be found in a casino, she thought with a droll observation of the fortunes on the table and the straying eyes on the faces.

Or him, she acknowledged as she brought her attention back to Giovanni and fell into the turbulent eyes of a creature far more dangerous than a shark. Not the merciless stare of a predator about to pounce, but the calculating intelligence of a man.

So compelling and so inscrutable.

"Do you mind if I go back to the room? Jet

lag is catching up to me." Along with a deep sense of inadequacy.

He refused to let her cross the street alone and escorted her to the penthouse. He was restless once they got there, though, not removing his jacket or tie. He picked up the card on the tray that held a bottle of scotch and read aloud, "Compliments of the management."

He tucked the card into his pocket and helped himself to a pour, but only held it without sipping. His tension was obvious.

"You're realizing that I'm as boring as I claim, aren't you?" She was trying to make light of it when she actually regretted being so frank. "You don't have to turn in because I am. If you want to go back and gamble, please do."

"I missed speaking to Clair's husband." He set aside his drink. "We have mutual business interests that I'd like to discuss with him. I won't be long."

It sounded perfectly reasonable, but for some reason her stomach clenched with suspicion. She wasn't sure why. It made her feel like a jealous girlfriend to have this lurching reaction when she had no reason to mistrust him. She had just urged him to go!

But she was stung that he was so quick to leave.

Everything felt very tenuous all of a sudden. The small connection they'd developed in New York was disintegrating, mostly because she was realizing exactly how far out of her reach he really was. Perhaps that sense of affinity had only ever been a conjured fantasy in her head anyway. She wanted to say, *Stay. Hold me.* But that seemed pathetic.

She made herself cross to set a hand on his shoulder. As she leaned to peck his mouth with a kiss, she murmured, "Good night."

He caught a firm hand around the back of her neck and held her for a long, possessive kiss that tasted of craving and frustration and conflict, further confusing her and leaving her breathless.

He reluctantly released her, gray eyes stormier than ever—which only reinforced her sense that something was amiss between them.

"I'll be back within the hour," he promised. "I'll try not to wake you."

She nodded and turned away, throat tight.

CHAPTER FIVE

"HAVE YOU LOST your mind?" was Everett's casual greeting when Giovanni let himself into the private salon with the card that had been propped against the bottle of scotch in his suite. "Why is she still with you? You're *working*."

Giovanni met the ice-blue eyes of his colleague. His boss, if one wanted to get technical. His *friend*, since there was no one else on earth who knew about this sideline job of his except the man who'd recruited him.

"The chancellor was there with his wife. His mistress was not, but he kept the napkin when his drink was delivered. The server was a brunette, midtwenties, five-eight or -nine with a mole on the left side of her throat. When she brought a scotch to the admiral, he tipped her *very* generously."

Everett sipped his drink, considering that in silence.

Everett had been born to a Swiss father who was a captain of automotive engineering and a French mother who translated at Interpol. He'd been at boarding school with Giovanni's brother and had come to the hospital often in that first year after the crash, as lost without his friend as Giovanni had been without his brother.

They had taken different paths for several years, but when Giovanni had uncovered a letter from a foreign government official attempting to blackmail his father into making certain concessions, he had realized it was evidence that his family had been murdered, not killed in a random crash as he'd always believed.

He hadn't known where to turn or who to trust, but given Everett's mother's connections, Giovanni had reached out to him.

That's when Everett had revealed he was more than the spoiled playboy he portrayed himself to be. He was employed by the American government and soon persuaded Giovanni to help him gather information and evidence for various ongoing investigations.

Giovanni had the ability to travel freely and infiltrate the highest industrial and political circles. It was amazing how nonthreatening a man in a wheelchair seemed to most people, or how quickly they opened up if they thought they could earn a favor from a wealthy man.

Giovanni had latched on to the challenge and inherent danger—Freja had read him correctly. There was an indescribable thrill in undercover work, avoiding detection while subversively righting wrongs and cleaning house at the highest level.

That side of his nature had made her uncomfortable, though, which left him questioning how badly he wanted to keep doing it.

"What of the waitress in *your* life?" Everett asked idly.

"You tell me," Giovanni challenged, hackles instantly rising. "Have you found anything?"

"No." Everett's mouth twisted with dismay. "All her income streams are legit. The monitoring of her tutoring hasn't turned up anything except one young man who is faking bad grades so he can keep paying her to talk to him. You have competition for her affections."

Giovanni didn't find that funny. At all.

"I told you she was harmless."

"Harmless?" Everett scoffed. "In less than twenty-four hours after approaching one of my most valued and highly placed operatives, she was in your bed. She hasn't left it. I'm not suggesting that chair means you're dead from the waist down, but this is completely out of character for you. If she was the corn-fed milkmaid she resembles, I wouldn't bat an eye, but she spent two years in *North Korea* and came out without a scratch. *How?*"

"Have you read her book?" Giovanni had finished it on the plane and Freja couldn't be more wrong, calling herself boring. She was resourceful and resilient. Kind and warmly funny. Infinitely fascinating.

"Have I read a lengthy fairy tale that pro-vides a comprehensive cover story for a sleeper agent? Yes. It stretches credulity. Her father could still be alive there. The authori-ties could be using him as leverage to keep her in line. Or holding those people she lived with. You can't risk having such a dark horse shadowing your every move. Send her back to New York," Everett ordered.

He debated briefly, then admitted, "I can't. We're waiting to see if she's pregnant."

Everett choked on his scotch.

"Screw you," Giovanni bit out. "I can get a woman pregnant."

Maybe. Hell, he didn't know, but from the

moment he'd realized there was a chance Freja might be carrying his baby, there was no question in him as to how he wanted to proceed. Of course she would stay with him. Of course he would marry her if a baby was on the way.

His reaction was primal and immediate, but he hadn't given thought to how that would look long-term, not until their odd conversation this evening when she'd pointed out how ill-suited she thought they were.

She was afraid to be tied to him by the child they might share. *Financial security is important, but I'm talking about emotional security.*

His ego was stung by the suggestion he would fail to provide everything she needed, but emotions were something he no longer used—like shoes.

"I wasn't questioning your ability." Everett gave a last cough into his fist. "I'm astonished you let her maneuver you into that risk. Can you be sure it's yours? You've known her less than a week."

"Screw you again. I'm not a victim. Sometimes things happen." The details were none of Everett's damned business. "I'm man enough to take responsibility for my own lapse in judgment so I will."

"Are you? Because this is sounding like a very big lapse." Everett was referring to more than a skipped condom. He meant getting involved with Freja at all.

"You've been doing this too long if you regard an innocent woman with this much cynicism, Everett."

"This cynicism keeps me and my people alive. You're one of my people, Giovanni, so appreciate it."

"Warm and fuzzy as that sounds, not everyone lives in this cloak-and-dagger world we occupy. *She* doesn't," Giovanni asserted.

"Yes, we do. *You* do." Everett sat on the edge of the sofa cushion, leaning forward. "If she is an innocent bystander, you're putting her in danger. If your cover is blown, she becomes a target. Do you realize that?"

"Of course I realize that!" Giovanni gripped the rims of his wheels so hard he should have bent them. "If she's not pregnant, I'll send her back to New York," he conceded in a snarl.

"That's the first intelligent thing you've said since you came in here." Everett sat back again. "What are you going to do if she is?"

"Marry her," Giovanni answered without hesitation. "And retire."

Everett swore. "I'll hope this is a false alarm, then."

Giovanni headed to the door aware he should be hoping the same thing. But he wasn't.

Despite her best efforts to quiet her misgivings and fall asleep, Freja was wide awake when Giovanni came to bed.

"Did you speak to him?" she asked.

He stilled with the covers still lifted by his upraised arm. "Who?"

"Aleksy."

"Oh. No." He finished settling on his back beside her. "He was tied up with someone else."

It was dark. She couldn't see his expression and he was a master at keeping any sort of emotional tells from his voice, but somehow that brisk "don't ask" tone left an impression that he wasn't being honest. She didn't know what the truth was, but that wasn't it.

A fault line cracked through her heart, leaving the two pieces offset in her chest. Which scared her. She had been lying there thinking about how quickly and deeply involved they'd become, trying to convince herself it was an entanglement that had more to do with logistics and sex than her heart, but this sudden, acute ache wouldn't be happening if she wasn't falling for him in a more profound way.

Should she challenge him? What was the point? If he wanted to tell her the truth, he would already be doing so.

"Why are you still awake?" he asked. "I thought you were tired."

"I am, but I can't stop thinking," she murmured.

"About?"

When she hesitated to answer, he rolled to face her and dragged her into the spoon of his body, his bulky warmth at her back something she'd been missing as she lay here alone.

"You're not boring," he growled. "You're witty and intelligent. So self-possessed I forget you're actually quite young and new to intimate relationships."

"Well, that's it exactly. What if we wind up married and we don't even know who we're married to?"

"We'll cross that bridge when we get to it. Do you want me to help you sleep?" He nuzzled his lips through her hair against her nape.

Oh, he knew exactly how easily that caress distracted her. A pleasurable shiver slid down her back while his hand shifted the silk of her nightgown against her stomach.

"I believe that involves keeping me awake a little longer." Nevertheless, her hips wiggled an instinctive answer, nudging deeper into the bend of his body, seeking the growing firmness she found there.

He made a noise of satisfaction and stroked his hand down her hip and thigh, then gathered her nightgown against his wrist as he came back up. His light touch grazed the damp hairs between her thighs and lingered to explore deeper, making her draw a breath of deep longing.

Another rumble of erotic gratification vibrated his chest against her back.

"This is why you can't sleep, *tisoru*." He stroked his fingers into the growing moisture, bringing her to vibrant, gasping life. "I'll be back. Stay right here." He rolled away and she heard the drawer as he retrieved a condom.

Moments later, he settled behind her again. The thick shape of him prodded where she was swollen with longing.

"I feel weak," she said on a small sob as her

body easily took him in. "You haven't even kissed me yet."

"I will." His stubbled chin moved the hair from her neck, and he opened his mouth against her skin. "I'll kiss you here if you need it." He drew her thighs apart, bracing her leg atop his thigh so she was open to his touch as he traced where his stiff shape filled her. "Tell me what you want. I'll give you anything."

"This," she breathed helplessly as she guided his caress. "I want this."

"Mmm. *Paradisu*," he agreed, taking his time with his luxurious explorations, not moving within her, but growing her arousal in increments while he dabbled kisses up her neck and suckled her earlobe. "Anytime you worry whether we will get along, think of how perfectly we fit like this, hmm?"

"I can't think," she said with a fractured breath. "You make me—" She gasped with shock at how quickly climax engulfed her.

He firmed his touch so he impaled her as deeply as he could while she shivered in orgasm. He hissed with pleasure at the way she convulsed in his arms.

Then he spoke only Sicilian, tone filled with praise as he stroked her all over, still barely shifting within her while he brought her to another peak of arousal before he joined her in the blinding ecstasy of release.

The next week passed in a blur. Freja enjoyed the mornings. She often joined Giovanni during his swim or physical therapy workout. Their breakfast was usually private. They would banter about the latest headlines and plan the rest of the day.

The rest of the day was mildly hellish. He would disappear for meetings while she was sent for fittings and spa treatments. Perhaps he thought he was spoiling her, but she didn't love strangers playing with her feet or using tweezers on her brows. Long nails made it hard to type and the polish made her feel vaguely suffocated.

Evenings were tolerable if lengthy events ranging from cocktail parties to white-tie galas. After the first two, Giovanni said, "You're very good at this."

"Talking to people? So are you. Everyone says you're so charming, but I've noticed all you do is coax them to talk about themselves. Sneaky."

He didn't laugh. He fixed her with his

sharpened gaze and noted, "You spoke with the countess a long time. What about?"

"Horses."

Giovanni wanted to know more. He nudged her along until she had relayed every word she'd exchanged with the pleasant if self-important woman.

"I didn't realize you were so into dressage." Was he *interested* in that other woman? "You should have joined us."

He must have heard the spark in her tone, but only said, "I thought you might have had a chance to mention your book. She does go on, though, doesn't she?" He changed the subject.

His curiosity stayed with her, feeding the tiny uncertainties in her that a dynamic man who had his pick among all these well-bred heiresses could remain interested in her.

A few days later, they had an even more disturbing encounter. They were in Frankfurt and Giovanni left to meet with automotive engineers. Freja was booked for a massage and a facial, but the sun was shining and she decided a walk along the river would relax her more.

She wound up crossing the Eiserner Steg, the iron footbridge. She was leaving a coffee shop, considering a visit to the museum up the block, when she saw Giovanni come out of it.

Her first instinct was to rush up and catch him. His car was pulling up to the curb, but two steps into her trot, she halted as it occurred to her that he might be with someone—a woman?

He moved toward the black sedan alone. The driver opened the door and Giovanni took one casual glance down the block, as anyone might.

He stiffened. They were a full block away, but she could tell he saw her. She knew he could see that she was staring at him, but there was that split second when he almost pretended he didn't see her and considered leaving.

She stood there with her feet rooted by confusion. Betrayal. Absorbing that he had *definitely* lied to her this morning about where he was going.

He said something to his driver and swiveled his chair, rolling toward her. After a second, she managed to stumble forward, then stop at the corner and wait for the light. She met him on the opposite corner.

"What are you doing here?" was his crisp greeting, as if she was the one off course. He looked at the coffee in her hand then glanced behind her. "Are you meeting someone?"

"No. Are *you*?"

"No. How did you get here? You're supposed to be in the spa."

Supposed to be?

"I felt like a walk."

"You *walked* from the hotel? You need to text me when you decide to go out alone. What if you got lost or something happened to you?"

"Are you serious? I was seven when my father taught me to avoid the streets where girls in heavy makeup and short skirts stand on corners. The only crime in this district is how much they charge tourists for coffee." She lifted her biodegradable cup. "Maybe *you* should text *me*, since you seem to be the one who's lost."

Oh, this man knew how to use a stare to slice and dice. "Let's get in the car. I'll take you back to the hotel."

"No, thank you. I feel like visiting the museum." She really didn't. "Perhaps you'd like to join me? Oh, you've already been, haven't you? Shame."

"Don't turn this into something it's not," he said in a withering voice. "I had a few minutes to kill before my meeting. The display on the history of the financial sector is interesting. Use my ticket. You can probably get in for free." He offered it to her.

She wanted to throw her coffee in his face. She marched past him.

"Freja!" he bit out through gritted teeth.

They pivoted to face one another, a handful of paces apart, like duelists.

"It was nothing," he said quietly. "Go in and ask around. People will remember if the man in the wheelchair was with anyone. I wasn't. We're fighting over nothing."

It didn't feel like nothing. Her chest was ready to burst with pressure. Her eyes were hot, but dry.

"We'll go in together." He came toward her.

"I don't even want to go. Not anymore." She looked back in the direction of the footbridge. It had been covered in love locks and she'd indulged a fantasy where she and Giovanni placed one. She should have been thinking about looking up flights to New York.

"If you're having second thoughts, just tell me," she said, refusing to play games.

He flinched. "I'm not."

"Because I told you we weren't suited for each other. I'd rather you were up-front—"

"I am not having second thoughts," he repeated firmly. "This isn't remotely what you're thinking." He sent a frustrated look toward the museum entrance. "Look, I'll walk with you. You're right. It's a nice day. We should enjoy it."

"What about your meeting?" she asked with suspicion.

"I'll cancel it." He took out his phone, sent a text and pocketed it again. Then he waved at his driver, signaling he didn't need him.

She stood there searching his expression, trying to process this about-face.

As he met her gaze, his shoulders lost some of their starch.

"I've been alone for a long time," he said without heat. "I've been making decisions for myself since I was fifteen. Major ones, like whether to have my own leg amputated." He waved at his stumps. "Answering to someone else does not come naturally."

He turned his chair and jerked his head to indicate she should walk with him.

"Telling people to fall in line is perfectly natural, however," she said, still sullen, but walking alongside him.

"It's like I was born for it," he said dryly.

"I didn't know that about your leg," she

said after they'd crossed the street and were heading back to the river walk. "You don't have any relatives? A guardian who could have helped you with that decision?"

For a second, she thought he would do that thing where he deflected and turned everything on her. Instead he said, "I have some aunts and uncles who did what they could, but they had their own families. We weren't close because my father had traveled so much I'd rarely seen them. I kept up on my schooling with a tutor and when I was discharged, it was more convenient all around to send me back to boarding school. It was already wheelchair-accessible and there were nurses to monitor my health, physical education staff to assist with therapy and my athletic aspirations."

"What about school holidays?"

"I usually had a competition somewhere or I just stayed and trained. It was only a year before I moved on to university and would have left home anyway."

"It still seems—"

"Don't call me sad."

"I wouldn't dare," she mumbled against the lid of her coffee.

She caught his mouth twitch. He was a tiny bit amused.

The river walk was paved and offered lovely views of the water and abundant greenery between the buildings. She paused to take a photo of the skyline on the opposite bank.

"Did you come here with your father?"

"On this walk exactly? At least four times." She looked at the image, decided to take one more. "To the city, probably a dozen. If we're counting passing through airports and train stations, so many times I couldn't tell you. I took a photo of myself on the footbridge today, to match one he took of me for one of his earliest books. Oliver and my agent have suggested I follow in his footsteps. They said I could offer some of his most popular destinations a 'then and now' treatment, with the contemporary twist of a woman striking out on her own. This was my first stab at it, to see if I like it or if it makes me miss him too much."

"And?"

"Both. It's nostalgic, but makes me melancholy, too. I'll see what kind of hits I get on the blog, but I already know people prefer more colorful places like Marrakesh."

"You are not going to travel alone."

She sipped her cooling coffee. "Why not? Do you ever travel for pleasure? Or is it always business?"

One of those unreadable shields slid over his expression. "One could argue you haven't traveled for pleasure, given it was your father's occupation."

She sighed at that enormously typical deflection.

He heard it. "I don't like talking about myself, Freja."

"Is it too personal to ask why not?" she asked snippily.

"Because I have to give up enough personal information as it is." He gave his wheels an impatient push as they reached a slight incline. "I have to let people touch me as though I'm a dog at the vet. They take blood and write down what I'm eating and whether I'm following instructions. They're only trying to help, I know that, but it's still a loss of dignity, especially when they ask me to do something and I have to say I can't. And you wouldn't believe the things that perfect strangers have the gall to ask because I'm down here at the height of a child."

"Am I allowed to be mad on your behalf?"

"Don't waste your energy. But I'll have a sip of that coffee."

They passed it back and forth as they continued along.

"I won't pretend I'm an easy man, Freja. I will continue to be arrogant and uncommunicative, but I will never cheat on you. I promise."

He sounded so sincere, she had to believe him.

Giovanni was more careful over the next few days. By the time they settled into his penthouse in Paris, things between him and Freja had returned to what passed as their normal, but Everett was right. Much as Giovanni hated to admit it, this wasn't sustainable. The mere thought of sending her back to New York had him tensing his arm around her, though, accidentally waking her.

She drew a deep breath and stretched, warm curves shifting against his side while her hand made a lazy pass across his chest.

"Did I fall asleep? I didn't mean to," she said in a murmur and snuggled back into him, thigh coming up to his waist and lips turning into his shoulder. Her hair tickled under his jaw and her breath warmed his skin as she said, "We have to go out tonight, don't we?"

"We have time." He played his fingers in her hair, bordering on addicted to this simple pleasure of having her naked in bed beside him, all sated and warm as they dozed off their sex.

Ah, the sex. That wicked, exalted act that had gotten him into this predicament.

"Freja?" He discovered his voice wasn't nearly as steady as it should be. He cleared his throat. "When do you expect to know if you're pregnant?"

Just like that, the equilibrium they'd found after that difficult day in Frankfurt was sucked away, leaving a silence so profound, he could hear his own heartbeat in his ears.

"I'm a day late," she said in a small voice.

His heart lurched so hard, the sound in his ears kicked to life like a furnace bursting into action on a shot of fuel. His whole being was accosted by euphoria.

"A day," he repeated with wonder.

"Only one. It doesn't mean—"

"I know." He touched her lips to silence her. "Let me have this." He had told himself it wouldn't matter, that it was such a long shot he shouldn't project any anticipation into it, but he closed his eyes to savor this moment of possibility.

"You can't *want* me to be pregnant," she said against his finger.

"Why can't I?" He opened his eyes and tucked his chin to look at her, combing her hair off her face with his hand. "Who wouldn't want a little girl with your disarming blue eyes? Or a boy with my stubborn personality annoying the hell out of me? Or the other way around?" He closed his fist in the tails of her hair and drew it beneath her chin, tilting her mouth up close enough to set a kiss on her lips. "If nothing changes overnight, I'll book you a doctor's appointment in the morning. I want to know."

"I bought a test while I was out today."

Another thrust of shock went through him, this one edged with irritation that she was continuing to wander cities without mentioning where she was going or who she was with. Everett was the suspicious one, but Giovanni didn't need these slivers of doubt.

"Did you take it?" he asked.

"No. It's still early. It might give a false negative."

"Is there such a thing as a false positive?"

"Not really."

"Then—"

Sudden tears welled in her eyes. "*Please*, can I wait until tomorrow?"

Emotion tightened his chest. He wrapped his arms around her and tucked her head back under his chin. "If that's what you want."

He couldn't stop the race of his heart, though, as he contemplated what might be.

She pressed her hand to his chest and drew back, blinking up at him with amazement. "You're excited. You really do want me to be pregnant."

"So much that I'm afraid you'll run screaming. And I can't chase you," he said wryly.

"You're the most confounding man." She dipped her forehead against his jaw with a flummoxed laugh, then kissed his chin. "Okay, then." She rose and pulled on her light robe. "There are two in the box. If it says negative, I'll try again in a couple of days."

He came up on an elbow to watch her dig a purchase from her bag and disappear into the bathroom.

How long was he supposed to wait? He heard the toilet flush and water run. The silence after that was too much for him. He moved into his chair and went to the door, knocked.

"It's open," she said faintly.

He pushed in to see her sitting on the edge of the tub. There were tears and a wobbling smile on her face.

All the air was punched out of his lungs. He clumsily bumped his way closer and looked at the faint lines on the stick.

"I've never thought of myself as a lucky person, but…" The tears on her lashes were catching the light like glitter. "I feel really, really lucky right now."

"Me, too. Come here." He held out his arms and she scooted into his lap.

He didn't know how to process the awe that gripped him. It was too big. Bigger than anything he'd ever experienced.

"Marry me," he said.

She bit her trembling lips and nodded shyly.

CHAPTER SIX

Present day

FREJA SWAM THROUGH piles of rustling silk to sit up, fighting to catch her balance as the vehicle made a few quick turns. She grasped the armrest on the door to steady herself and flashed a malevolent look at Giovanni.

"I want a divorce."

"Lock the doors," Giovanni said to the driver as his incisive glance landed on her hand where she gripped the door.

The hard click of the door locks sounded and the SUV slowed for a light.

"Put your seat belt on," Giovanni instructed her.

She conjured her filthiest look. She didn't want him dead, not in her heart of hearts. She wasn't that kind of person. But with her eyes she urged, *Die.*

He released a short-tempered sigh and started to unclick his own belt.

She shot up a staying hand to hold him off and resentfully buckled herself. She refused to look at him. Not when he was over there oozing even more sex appeal than ever with that scruffy beard and his massive shoulders straining the fabric of his black hoodie.

She gave the catch of the door a useless, furious pull and let it thunk back into place.

"I know you're angry," Giovanni said in a tight voice, as though it pained him to say it. "You have a right to be."

"Do I?" Her choke of disbelief nearly spat her tongue onto the floor. What a colossal understatement! "It's so nice of you to give me permission to have feelings. Do you know what I give *you* permission to do? Only two guesses since it's only two words."

"You're not that surprised to see me, Freja. You knew I wasn't dead."

"Oh, that makes it all better then." She yanked every last inch of her skirt onto her side of the seat, gathering it all into her lap so not one stray bead or thread touched him.

"I was in a coma—"

"Until *today*?" She was being sarcastic, but concern clawed through her, forcing her to look at him. His color was good and he seemed as vital and healthy as always.

"For a week," he allowed. "Someone was trying to kill me. Everett—" he nodded at the man before him in the passenger seat "—had to make a decision about whether to let them believe they'd succeeded. There were other factors that kept me in hiding after that."

One week. That was the only thing that Freja processed. He'd been unconscious for one week. He must have known she'd been in hospital herself, but hadn't made an effort to come.

She looked out the window again, refusing to let him see her tears. She swallowed back the agony that ached in her throat, ready to choke to death on it before she let him see how badly he could still hurt her.

"If they'd known I was alive, you would have become a target." Giovanni was using that awful tone that urged her to be reasonable. "I'll explain when we get where we're going."

"Don't bother. I don't care," she lied, looking at her small reflections in the sunglasses he was wearing. "You might not be dead, but anything I ever felt for you is. You feel the same or you would have turned up sooner."

"I'm here now."

"Yes, and I was assured it would be a quick, clean, no-fuss conversation to pick you up," Everett said with a testy smile over his shoulder. "Why did you run?"

"Gosh, I don't know. Fear of kidnapping?"

Despite the insulated interior, the sound of a siren penetrated. Before she could crane her neck to see whether it was the police and if they were in pursuit, the SUV ducked into the underground parking garage of a skyscraper. It stopped beside an open elevator flanked by two lean bodyguards.

Everett and the driver got out. The door was still locked beside her. She tried it despite the fact that the driver stood on the other side, ensuring she wouldn't get very far even if she managed to exit that side.

"I'm taking you to my safe house," Giovanni said. "We'll talk there."

"No, thank you." She curled her hand around the strap of her seat belt where it crossed her chest.

The back of the SUV opened and Everett removed Giovanni's wheelchair, then slammed it shut again.

"Look around you, Freja. You *are* coming with me. I'd rather it was your choice."

"Are you listening to yourself? You're not giving me one."

"I'm not asking you to forgive me, only to trust me that this was necessary. For both of our safety."

Her vision blurred with instant, furious tears. Helpless anguish. "I can *never* trust you. Do you realize that? How could you even suggest it?"

"Have I ever hurt you?" he demanded tightly, then swore and looked away, seeming to realize as he said it that he was inviting the vitriol that climbed like bile into her throat. "I meant physically. Look, I've been waiting for the right time to resurface. I need to know you're safe when word gets out that I'm alive. As of today's debacle, it's out. Please come with me and let me explain."

She realized the ache in her other hand was from gripping her phone this whole time. All those people inside this tiny rectangle, all those "friends" who'd been so sympathetic, eating up her grief like bitter chocolate bonbons. Where were they now, when she was in real trouble? *Not here.*

She fingered her pendant, thinking of Nels. He was a reliable friend, but they weren't exactly soul mates.

She didn't have anyone. That's what she'd come to terms with since Giovanni's disappearance. For a few short months, Giovanni had encouraged her to believe they were a unit. The kernels of a small and growing family.

That fantasy had vanished as quickly as it had formed.

"I'll go if you promise you'll divorce me. I'm not staying married to you."

A pause, then, "If that's what you want, but we might have to wait a few weeks."

"I'm not sleeping with you," she blurted.

"I don't expect you to."

As his flat response struck like an anvil, splitting her down the middle like a chunk of redwood, she realized she had been hoping for more of a fight. Apparently, that's not what this was.

The void of sorrow that had consumed her since his "death" closed in like a fog. Probably for the best. Giovanni had caused her too much emotional upheaval as it was. They needed closure and a clean break. Then she would finally stop crying over him. She would be able to speak without powdered glass in her throat. To breathe one breath that wasn't so heavy with loss it nearly crushed her flat.

"Take your money back, too," she said distantly. "I don't need it and it's just one more headache I don't want to deal with."

"Anything else?"

Oh, he thought he could take that sardonic tone with her? She blinked fast to see him through her matted lashes.

"Take off that ring. It's a mockery that you're wearing it."

"You want to talk about mocking our marriage with what we're wearing?" His pithy tone disparaged the meringue confection piled around her. "I promised you I would put it back on and never remove it again. I won't break that vow. So no, I will not take it off." He rapped a knuckle on the window and the locks were released. "Let's go."

Giovanni felt the familiar *tink* of metal to metal, his wedding ring grazing his hand rim as he rolled his wheelchair aboard the customized, unmarked, military-grade helicopter. He anchored his chair into its spot next to her seat.

He had insisted Everett retrieve the ring the minute he was conscious enough to comprehend all that had happened. He'd promised Freja he would put it back on his finger and never remove when she'd caught him without it. That had been minutes—twenty or thirty at most—before the explosion that had "killed" him.

Freja was watching Everett come in behind them and start to take the seat across from her. Her stiff profile was unnaturally ashen, not a version of her typical ivory skin tone, and not the clean, snowy white of her gown. She looked like bone china—delicate and translucent.

"Everett." Giovanni jerked his head toward the door.

Everett's face tightened, but Giovanni didn't relent. *Get me that ring and I'll do everything you ask.* He had. For three months he'd played dead, allowing Everett to identify the mole who'd set him up. That was over now. Giovanni had bought his freedom fair and square.

His promise to stay off grid had been a small bluff in the first place since he couldn't exactly hike out of the mountains on his nonexistent feet, but he would have turned himself into the most intractable asset anyone could have imagined if Everett hadn't done as he asked.

If I steal that ring and only that ring, she

could become suspicious and deduce that you're alive.

That had been Giovanni's goal.

"I'll catch the next one, then," Everett said with caustic mockery.

"Collect Freja's things from her hotel," Giovanni suggested. "Settle up at the wedding shop. I'm sure they'll have questions."

Everett muttered something as he rose, but Giovanni had higher priorities than to worry about Everett's disgruntled cleanup of the mess his wife had made.

The doors closed and they were alone in the small cabin.

Freja nervously turned the flashy engagement ring she wore.

The dress, the diamond ring, the heart emojis beneath the professional engagement photos… Giovanni had seen all of her effusive posts as the acts of war she intended them to be. Every single one had landed like mortar shells in the middle of his angry, aching heart.

They'd both been wildly happy and gut-wrenchingly miserable in those weeks between their quickie wedding and their final confrontation. He had thought those strained days had been the limits of hell he could endure. He'd been proven so wrong.

"I should have come with you that day," Giovanni said gravely. Humbly.

Around and around the ring was going, faster and faster. "You sent me to your room to wait like a child."

He'd been in unstoppable agony over how badly he'd handled that day. Impatience had been driving him. He hadn't wanted to wait for Everett's latest reports on the contacts he'd made. He'd wanted all of this over so he could properly devote himself to his marriage.

He'd taken a stupid risk and paid the price.

"I was coming after you. That's why I survived. I was supposed to meet someone, but it was a setup. The café was completely empty except for explosives, not that I knew it. After our argument, I suspected you wouldn't wait for me. I started back to the hotel instead of going in. When I turn to leave, they panicked and hit the detonator. Since I wasn't in the center of the blast, I only suffered a few broken bones and a concussion."

"And a coma." She kept her chin tucked as she sent him an appalled look, the first sign of concern he'd seen.

"Induced. They were worried about my spine. Once the swelling went down, they brought me out. By then, Everett had pronounced me dead."

He waited for her to say she was glad he'd survived, but he had a grim sense he would wait a long time to hear those words, if he ever did.

She folded her hands in her lap, very much the contained, enigmatic Freja he knew so well. She'd been kidnapped by her resurrected husband and she only wore a pinched thoughtfulness around her white lips and had her brow furrowed in thought.

The most hysteria she'd revealed today had been the moment when Everett had approached them as Giovanni had pulled her into the back of the SUV. Her fists had clenched into Giovanni's hoodie, whether seeking protection or refusing to be torn from him he didn't know, but he held tight to that instinctive reaction, desperate for it to mean she still felt something for him despite her claims to the contrary.

"I walked into that hotel room and saw the ring and I was so angry." Her voice panged. "I took it and left. Walked outside and a couple from Tuscany was leaving to catch the ferry back to Italy." Her voice grew dull and so empty he felt the cavernous chill in his chest as she continued. "When we got to the slip, everyone was talking about the blast. I realized it had happened close to where I'd seen you and tried calling. People were tweeting. There was a picture of a wheelchair lying in the street."

"Freja." He tried to take her hand.

She shook her head, elbows tight to her ribs, voice choking up. "I went to the hospital and was told a man with no legs had been brought to it, but he was expected to survive. Then someone else pulled me aside and said you were dead, but they wouldn't let me see you."

"If I had been conscious, I wouldn't have let them do that to you." Everett had been suspicious of her presence there, unsure who he could trust until he had Giovanni well away from the area and conscious enough to tell him what had happened.

"I guess I went into shock because I was lying in a bed when someone handed me a bag with your clothes and wallet and passport. I remember staring at it, saying I thought it had been the worst thing in the world that you weren't wearing your wedding ring when I saw you last. That man who'd brought it—he couldn't have been an orderly. I don't know who he was, but he was trying to be kind. He said you were wearing it. He swore he'd seen it himself, but said it couldn't be removed without cutting and ruining it. You would be cremated with it, he said, and he was sure you loved me very much."

Giovanni closed his eyes. "But you already had it."

"And all I could think was, *You liar.*" She gave a broken laugh. "I asked what sort of arrangements I had to make and they were already made. Your things showed up from the hotel and I was flown back to Rome. It was all so very trouble-free," she scoffed. "But when I unpacked your things, your little kit of fix-it tools wasn't there. Which didn't make *any* sense because I'd seen it on the dresser next to the ring. One of the little screwdrivers had been left out, as if you'd made a last-minute adjustment before you left. Who steals an old, beat-up pair of calipers and a little screwdriver set? Your wheelchair showed up, rim bent and one of the small wheels missing, but the one thing *you* bring almost everywhere with you wasn't there."

"So you knew even before I had Everett get the ring." He wouldn't call it a relief, but he had hated that she had been lied to. That she had suffered. "I wanted to tell you, Freja. The minute I woke up and realized, I wanted you to know I was alive. Other lives would have been at risk, including yours. Taking back this ring was the best message I could send while also keeping it subtle enough it could be dismissed as a robbery if you decided to tell anyone."

She was turning the engagement ring again.

"Will you take that off?" he requested.

"No."

"Why not?"

"Because I'm marrying someone else."

Less than an hour later, the helicopter descended into a remote valley flickering with the reds and golds of autumn.

"Where are we?" Freja asked.

"Near the Swiss border."

Seemingly out of nowhere, a structure came into her sightline as they touched down. The floor-to-ceiling windows were overhung with a long platform covered in foliage so the house had been mostly indiscernible from the ground. It was a modern mansion built into the mountainside overlooking the snake of a silver river in the valley bottom.

The rotors stopped and Giovanni went out ahead of her.

A trim middle-aged man with a crisp white tunic over dark blue pants waited with a woman of similar age. Their smiles faltered with surprise when Freja emerged in her massive gown.

"Freja, this is Kurt. He's my physical therapist. His wife, Marie, is a registered dietician and keeps the house."

"Nice to meet you," Freja said with as much warmth as she could muster, shaking their hands. "I wonder if I could borrow a change of clothes?" she asked Marie.

"There's a full selection in the guest room," Marie said. "And fresh coffee and cake."

"We'll serve ourselves," Giovanni said. "Take some downtime."

The couple disappeared down a set of stairs to a lower floor of the pseudo-mansion.

"You've been staying here this whole time?"

"Yes."

The location was incredibly beautiful. Private and peaceful with only the sound of birdsong and rustling leaves now that the helicopter had fallen silent. A light breeze carried a hint of autumn briskness, but the air tasted of forests and streams and earthy wildness.

Freja followed Giovanni up the gradual incline of a covered zigzag path. She gave up trying to keep the dress pristine and only picked up the front of the skirt so she wouldn't trip, letting the rest drag behind her as she followed him to the veranda. A small dining table looked up the valley, and a collection of cushioned outdoor furniture was positioned around an unlit fire bowl.

Giovanni slid open the screen door into the house. The wide entrance easily accommodated his chair. The sill of the door was recessed so he didn't even bump across it. Inside, the open-plan living area was arranged as most of his properties were, with airy spaces between the furniture. The kitchen had two sinks, one for standing, one for sitting, with room against the lowered counter to accommodate his chair. Since the house was built into the mountainside, the upper cupboards had translucent panels in the doors with lights behind to give the impression of sunlight coming in from that angle.

"When did you have this built?" It couldn't have been thrown together within the last few months, not with this much tasteful attention to his specialized details.

"A few years ago. Before we met."

"It's not listed among your assets." She'd been through his portfolio of investments and properties umpteen times with Nels and lawyers and predators from his various corporate headquarters.

"As you guessed very quickly in our marriage, I lead—rather, I used to lead—it's over. I *led* a double life. About ten years ago, I discovered the crash that killed my family was deliberate. Someone had been trying to bribe my father. He refused so he was permanently removed from his post. Everett was a friend of Stefano's who had connections at Interpol. One thing led to another and I've been working with him ever since."

"Doing *what*?"

"Collecting intelligence."

"You're a *spy*?"

"That makes me sound as though I'm dropping from helicopters and kicking in doors. I talk to people, uncover hidden relationships and follow the money. If we're lucky, we compile enough evidence to expose corruption and make arrests."

She ought to be more incredulous, but it

fit so neatly into all the strange prevarications during their short marriage. The private calls and the disappearing for meetings that weren't on his calendar. Maybe she was latching on to the explanation out of relief. It was a damned sight better to hear he was a secret agent than a cheating husband.

"But if you had all this to hide…why did you marry me?"

"You know why we married," he said gruffly.

They were only a few feet apart, close enough to see each other's eyes. His were bleak and gathering with questions, but a gulf opened between them. A chasm. A wide, throbbing wound that pulsed painfully in her ears and stung her nostrils and scorched her throat.

She wasn't ready to talk about that. *Couldn't*.

"I mean, why did you let it get that far?" she choked. "Why even ask me to dinner? Why…?" He had brought her home and told her to be the sensible one that first night. She hadn't had the confidence to drag him into a relationship. He had pursued her. He must know he had!

A muscle pulsed in his jaw before he said without emotion, "The way we met, the fact you mentioned Stefano, seemed suspicious. You had a full dossier in the system."

"What system?"

"*The* system. You'd been questioned about your time in North Korea. Everett and I thought you might still have connections there."

"You thought *I* was a spy?" Now she was flabbergasted.

"It seemed possible. Everett thought—"

"I don't care what Everett thought! *You* thought I could be a secret agent? Is that right? You thought that *I* knew you were a spy and I targeted you? You thought I gave you my virginity, got *pregnant* and *married* you because I wanted to—what? Expose you? Pump you for information? I'm not that complicated! I just wanted—"

Her throat locked over a lump of emotion as she contemplated the dreams that had died between then and now.

"Freja." His voice was ragged, his brow pulled with torture.

"I want out of this dress."

Freja flung around, skirt swirling. The silk fluttered behind her as she sailed down the hall and found the guest room.

Giovanni stayed where he was, head tilted against the back of his chair. His eyes were closed, but he still saw her face. The betrayal in her eyes, the anguish around her mouth.

He reflexively tried to push that image into a mental vault along with the ache in his throat, but it didn't work.

From the time he'd woken seventeen years ago, after a car crash that left him nothing of the life he'd known, Giovanni had become very good at compartmentalizing. Rather than deal with the grief of losing his family, he focused on overcoming the physical pain of his recovery. Rather than resent his inability to live in his family home because it couldn't accommodate his wheelchair, he had focused on athletics that took him to far-off places. If his chair held him back from the wild pursuits of youth, he concentrated on making money. Doors were always thrown wide open for gold.

Then, when he took the reins of his father's business from the trustee and finally decided to face his past by going through old papers, he had found the evidence of attempted bribery.

Emotions had roared to life in him. Injustice. Hatred for the perpetrators. Intense bitterness at the personal injury he'd suffered for such paltry reasons as jockeying among energy sector bids. He should have blown open like a volcano. Instead, he had pushed all that emotion back inside him to use as fuel. He had gone to Everett and focused on proving the crime, naming names and dismantling that small tangle of venality.

Afterward, when he was still confronted with a life that was tormentingly empty, he had brushed aside any soul-searching and leaped on Everett's request for assistance with the next assignment and the next.

So he ought to be able to handle and dismiss the remorse he felt right now. He ought to be able to think past it and know what to do, but no matter how hard he tried to set aside his emotions, it didn't work. It had never worked with Freja. He had been sitting here for three months, tortured by what he was doing to her.

"Ahh!"

Her distressed scream had him flying down the hall to the closed door of the guest room.

"Freja." He yanked at the latch, surprised to find it unlocked, and pushed in.

She stood in the middle of the room, wild-eyed, face flushed and hair mussed.

Her hands were clenched in the edge of lace across the tops of her breasts.

"I can't get out of it." She fairly shook with rage.

"I thought you were being murdered." His limbs were shaking with the adrenaline that had sent him racing in here. He rolled in far enough to throw the door shut behind him. "Sit." He motioned to the corner of the bed.

She plopped down, back still heaving with exertion as she slumped with her elbows on her thighs and dropped her face into her hands.

For one second, he just looked. He drank in the sad slope of her shoulders, the fall of her scattered hair, her ivory skin and the bow of her back and the slip of a waist that was far too thin. The longing in him to pick her up and draw her into his lap was so intense he shook with the effort to resist it.

Very gently, he reached out to sweep her hair to the front of her shoulder, exposing her delicate nape. Dear God, he could live his entire life with his lips pressed to that sensitive spot that always made her quiver and sigh with bliss.

He wanted to pet his hand down her back, soothe her, draw her in. Make up and make love.

He forced himself to release the first tiny button, then the next. There were at least two dozen. It felt like hundreds, every single one too small for his big, clumsy fingers.

"You don't have to be so careful. It's ruined anyway."

There was a jealous, betrayed husband in him that wanted to rip this offensive dress right off her. How *dare* she spend his money on a dress for a wedding to another man?

But if he tore it in haste, he wouldn't be able to sit this close and watch that narrow strip of spine appear, would he? He wouldn't see her erratic breaths catch and her shoulder blades flex in reaction to his touch.

"Why all this pageantry if you knew you couldn't go through with the wedding?"

"I presumed if you let it happen then you really did plan to stay dead, so what did it matter if I was breaking the law? And my income depends on clicks, doesn't it? The bigger the dress, the higher the view count."

And the higher the chance he would see it? He allowed his fingertips to graze her warm skin.

She sat straighter, but he couldn't tell if that was reaction or rejection.

"Your blog says you knew him at school.

I thought all the men there were twits who failed to impress you?"

"I couldn't help being impressed by Nels. He's very intelligent, but was always very focused on his studies. Now that he's written the bar, he has time for a relationship."

"So you're sleeping with him." It made him sick.

She jerked to her feet and spun to confront him, catching at the gaping front of her dress. "Do you have the right to question me on whether I was faithful when you were pretending to be *dead*?"

He narrowed his eyes. "You knew I was alive. You knew we were still married."

"But I didn't know where you were or whether you would ever show your face again. You were dead *enough*. For all I knew, *you* were sleeping with other people."

"Kurt and Marie are not into swinging. Aside from them, Everett and the pilot—neither of whom is my type—are the only people I've seen between leaving hospital and getting you today."

"Poor you. I've had nothing but offers. It's amazing how alluring a woman is when she has a billion dollars to her name. Nels is the only man I trust these days. That includes you."

"So you're marrying him for protection?" Not love?

"No one was coming to save me, Giovanni. *You* weren't. I had to look after myself and I have." Her chin came up and scorched flags of anger sat on her cheekbones. "I guess I'm being unnecessarily modest. If you were interested in seeing any of this, you would have shown up sooner."

She dragged her dress down, exposing her braless breasts. The pale globes jiggled as she worked the gown past her hips and left it as a mound on the floor, like a pile of melted snow.

He stopped breathing as he ate up her lissome figure. His entire being came alive as though he was feeling sunshine for the first time after a decade in prison. Her beige underpants looked paper-thin. They hugged her hips from her navel to the tops of her thighs, seamless as yoga shorts. He wanted to touch them, feel her warmth through the fine silk.

She turned to a drawer and shook out a lemon-yellow T-shirt. She dropped it over her head, then stepped into a pair of jeans from the next drawer. They were a little loose. She'd definitely lost weight.

"Nels has probably seen the video." She

picked up her phone off the top of the dresser. "I should let him know I'm fine. What's the password to get online?"

"He'll see that you were with your husband. Since he's so intelligent, I'm sure he'll figure out the wedding is off."

She threw her phone onto the bed, temper instantly relit and now incandescent, beautiful in the way that the lightning strike that kills you fills you with awe at the same time.

"Or he'll activate the transmitter he suggested I wear because I'm worth a billion dollars and wanted to come to Europe alone." She picked up the pendant she wore around her neck.

How was he still underestimating her?

"Damn you, you always look so damned innocent and you're not!" He crashed his fist against his dead leg. "This is why I had to wonder if you were working for another government. You do these sly, underhanded things, hack my calendar and track my phone—yes, I know you did that. You followed me to Dubrovnik the very day I was nearly killed—"

"I thought you were having an affair!" she cried. "And that is a completely understandable suspicion when you were sneaking around as much as you were. You kept telling me you wanted to be a f—" She choked to a halt.

His heart clenched again, the way it had a few minutes ago in the lounge. He had never properly dealt with that pain because he didn't know how.

Freja turned away and flung open the drapes to reveal the glass doors that opened onto the fire escape. A full-spectrum bulb gave the impression of natural light, but it only led to a wide breezeway that terminated at the veranda.

"This is a stupid house!" She clattered open the door and stormed out.

CHAPTER SEVEN

FREJA HADN'T BOTHERED to put on socks or shoes. She was barefoot and even the paved passageway out of the bedroom had tiny pebbles that were sharp enough to cut into her soles. She didn't get very far on the cold path that wound down the hill.

With a huff, she stopped at the rail near the now empty helipad and brooded, rubbing one foot over the other to brush off the bottoms of her feet.

"I should have asked if you have any dietary restrictions," Marie said behind her.

Freja turned to see the woman was wearing gloves and a sunhat. She was pulling up plants in a small vegetable garden that was going to seed.

"I'm not fussy, but I'm not hungry right now, thanks."

Marie hesitated, then said, "It's nice to

meet you in person. I've read all of your father's books and really enjoyed them."

Freja scrounged up the smile she turned on for her father's fans. "Pappa would be pleased to know they entertained you."

"I usually prefer romance, but they were here and there's not much to do in the evenings except read, so—"

"They're here?" *Oh, that odious man.*

"In the study," Marie said, but Freja was already charging up the path as quickly as her bare feet would take her.

She burst into the study to find Giovanni speaking to his open laptop. "—ensure he knows she's safe and—"

Giovanni halted and Everett's voice asked sharply, "What is it?"

In one sweeping glance, Freja took in the hardwood floors that Giovanni preferred. He sat at one of the modern desks he seemed to order in bulk because they accommodated all his different types of chairs. There was a small reading area in the corner with a recliner and a standing lamp. Bookshelves bracketed golden drapes that she assumed disguised another of those weird emergency exits.

Freja marched over and sure enough, there

were all her father's titles in a tidy row at a convenient height to a man in a wheelchair. All the book jackets showed signs of wear, like library books that had been read several times.

"Giovanni," Everett prompted, but he was watching her.

She grabbed a handful and pulled them off the shelf, letting them tumble to the floor.

"I'll call you back," Giovanni said in a tone more weary than wary. "But yes, make that call and come for us in the morning. We'll return to Rome and have the press conference there." He closed the laptop. "Why are you angry that I have those?"

All of the books were hitting the floor with unsatisfying thumps. Year after year of her childhood, piling up after being consumed by him, secretly, over the last months.

"You could have asked *me*. How dare you hide out here, reading my dead father's words about me, rather than talk to me yourself? Do your covert information-gathering on anyone else on this earth, but not *me*."

"You looked me up online before I even knew you existed, Freja."

"I will never forgive you for any of this. Do you understand that?" She swept the last of the books onto the floor and stood there glaring at him.

"I know that!" he near-roared, temper snapping in a way that had her recoiling in shock. He had never yelled at her. Not once. "I knew it when I woke up and Everett told me he'd killed me." He snatched a book off his desk, one that had been set facedown, pages splayed open as though he'd been reading it minutes ago. "You think this has been easy for me?" He shook the book at her. *"This was all I had."*

"That was your choice!"

"No, it *wasn't*. For God's sake, Freja, step out of your own hurt and look at the big picture. Do you honestly think I would put both of us through all of this on a whim? People's lives were at stake. I got sloppy because I was impatient to retire from all of this." He threw down the book and pinched the bridge of his nose. "I've spent the last months thinking that if I'd only met you now, when I've done as much as I could, instead of when I was in the thick of an unfinished job, we might have had a chance. But I *am* out of it now. You and I can start fresh." His head came up. His gray eyes, dark as gathering thunderclouds, pierced into hers. "This is our chance for a new beginning, one that isn't overshadowed by anything in our past."

She shook her head. "Our past is going to follow us forever. I said I want a divorce and I meant it."

She spoke with guttural fervor, but it was reflexive defense. Fear of more pain. Even so, there was a faint flutter of hope in her that yearned for exactly what he was offering. She hadn't wanted to acknowledge it. That would mean he could hurt her anytime he wanted and she would forgive him for it. She couldn't do that.

Could she?

His expression tightened. He looked to his closed laptop.

"We will have to play the happy, reunited couple for the short term." There was no arguing with that implacable command. "I've been identified in the video and Everett is making some final arrests as we speak. You and I will both have to make statements. The helicopter is coming back in the morning."

Perversely, she was annoyed by that. She finally had him to herself and they were turning around and going back into the public eye? She crossed her arms and stared at the books tumbled around her feet. It had been childish to throw them around like that, but she was so angry. So filled with futility she had no means to express.

"You have always been a puzzle to me, Freja." He spoke more quietly. Gently. "You're completely unlike anyone else I've ever met. I was trying to understand you when I began reading those. If I hadn't had this double life, your quirks and contradictions wouldn't have fazed me, but you're this anomaly who picks up a language in minutes and moves through a foreign city as though you already know every street."

"I know I'm not normal!"

"Neither am I! That's what I'm saying." He sat back with a tired exhale and turned up a hand in a plea for understanding. "You slid past my very stalwart defenses the moment we met, made me your first lover on our first date. We happened *so fast*, Freja. You know that. I couldn't take you at face value, given what I was hiding. I had to keep my guard up."

"*You* made everything happen fast. That was your fault," she accused him, pointing at him.

"You didn't slow me down," he threw back.

"And that made me an object of suspicion?

I'm sorry for being attracted to you, okay? I thought you were a better man than you are. I won't make that mistake again."

A muscle pulsed in his cheek. "You're hurt so you're trying to hurt me. It's working." His gaze pierced into her, so naked for a second, she forgot to breathe. So anguished, the backs of her eyes grew hot. "I will accept all those stones you're hurling because at least you're here to hurl them."

Her bottom lip pushed up into her top, and she had to pull it between her teeth and bite to keep from letting a sob of pain escape her thick throat. She looked away, still angry, still hating him, but now hating herself a little, too.

"This is who we are, Freja. I've had ample time to reflect on that. We happened too soon, too fast. Too *hard*. Our timing was off and our feelings were too strong. I've walked through every single 'if only' and 'I should have.' The truth is, I wouldn't have done anything differently. I wanted you in my life, even though you weren't supposed to be there. There were times you could have made different choices, too, but you didn't. Because we're inevitable."

She rubbed where his words seemed to arrow straight into her heart.

"You go ahead and fight that as long as you need to. I tried, yet I'm still wearing this." He showed her the band on his finger. "But don't think any of this was what I wanted or that it came without a cost to me."

"So what am I supposed to do? Just be fine with all of this?" She waved around a wild hand, tears of betrayal and despair filling her eyes.

"Healing takes time. Not everything goes back to the way it was. I am intimately acquainted with that reality. But we can recover from this, Freja. And we can still have a very good life."

She shook her head. "I don't want to try."

He sucked in a breath as though she'd shot him, which gave her zero satisfaction as she walked out.

Part of him knew he was dreaming, but the flash of her yellow shirt disappearing into the trees was too real. Too terrifying.

In his head, he was thinking he should hit the intercom and tell Kurt to bring her back, but his wheelchair was rolling recklessly down the path at speeds he'd only attempted in races on well-swept trails. Yet not fast enough. She was already gone into the darkened woods.

"Freja!" Out of sheer frustration, he threw himself from his chair—

The ground rushed up to knock his breath from his body. His head glanced off the wheel of his chair where he'd left it by the nightstand. It burned like hell, but not as much as the ignominy of falling out of bed.

He swore roundly as he tried to orient himself, pushing to sit with his back against the side of the mattress, still sweating, heart pounding, trying to catch his breath.

"Giovanni?" Freja burst in and pulled up short in the doorway, backlit by the hall light.

He could only see the top half of her since he was on the floor on the far side of the bed. She wore a slinky nightgown as pale as her limbs. She came in a few more steps.

"Where are you?"

How humiliating. "Here. On the floor."

"What happened? Are you hurt?" She came around the end of the bed.

"Sir?" Now Kurt was here. Fantastic.

"I'm fine," Giovanni growled. "Go back to bed."

"I'll call you if we need anything," Freja

told Kurt as she shooed him from the door and closed it. "Do you want help?" she asked.

"I don't need help getting back into bed, Freja."

"I didn't ask if you needed help. I asked if you wanted it. You did call me," she pointed out in a huffy voice.

"And you came?" His scathing tone prompted a profound silence.

"So you don't want me."

"That is a loaded question and you know it." He dropped his head against the mattress. "Do I want you in my bedroom? Yes. A thousand times, yes. Do I want you witnessing my clumsiness? No."

There was a long silence and he sensed her hovering by the door as though trying to work out how to react.

He hadn't moved off the floor. The hardwood was unforgiving through his boxer briefs, the bar of the bedframe digging into his back. Nothing about this moment was comfortable, so he made it even less so.

"I dreamed you were running away. I was trying to come after you."

He heard her swallow. She moved to perch on the chair in the corner.

"I was lying awake thinking about it," she

admitted. "I'm so angry with you, I don't know what to do with it all. I've never been a person who wants revenge, but you're right. I want to hurt you in every possible way." She didn't sound angry. She sounded profoundly sad.

He closed his eyes, defeated by a circumstance that had snowballed so far beyond his ability to control, it was no wonder she'd been flattened by it.

"Do you want me to put on the light?" she offered.

"No." This was safer. He quit sulking and rolled onto his good leg, able to lever himself up enough he could grab a handful of blankets and drag himself back onto the bed. He adjusted his briefs and sat on the edge of the mattress, trying to read her pale expression in the faint glow from the nightlight in the bathroom.

"You're never clumsy," she murmured. "I'm always amazed at your strength and agility. You're like a gymnast."

"Will you come here?" He pushed aside the bunched blankets and patted the edge of the bed. "It's not a trick. I just want to ask you something."

She rose and drifted toward him like a

wraith, unafraid despite the swamp of percolating emotions between them.

"So trusting," he murmured as she lowered to sit beside him.

"I've always felt safe with you. That's why I'm so angry. I didn't believe you would hurt me, but you did."

"*Is* that why you're angry?" He picked up her hand and threaded his fingers through her slender, twitching ones. "Or is it something else? Tell me what happened, Freja."

She gasped and tried to jerk back her hand, but he held on even when she rose and tried to pull away.

"Is that why you called me in here?" She gave her hand a firmer tug.

He kept his hold gentle, using two hands to trap hers in a careful cage, but, "I have to know, Freja."

"You didn't want to know when it happened," she choked, roughly trying to shake him off. "I don't owe you any explanations now."

"No, you don't. But I'd like to understand." His heart was throbbing, the dull ache that had been in him for months pounding like hammers of fire driving icy spikes into his heart. "Sit," he coaxed. "Take your time."

She stood with her hand limp in his, face turned to the window, her profile ashen and still. For a long time, there was only the faint sound of their unsteady breaths.

Finally, she said in a voice that echoed with loss, "I went for a scan and they said she wasn't developing properly."

"She." He had to consciously keep himself from crushing the fine bones of her hand, but his hold on her firmed, as though he could keep her from being dragged into the pit of pure agony he heard in her voice. She was pulling him into it with her, though, and he feared they would never emerge because he had to ask, "Was it anything to do with me? Because of—"

"No." Her voice was shredded with pain. "I asked if it was because I'd been under stress and they said it was no one's fault. Just bad luck."

There was no comfort in that. It was still an abysmal sorrow.

"They said I could terminate or let nature take its course. They sent me home to think about it, but that night it started to happen and I went to hospital until it was over."

"I'm so sorry, Freja."

"No, you're not." She bitterly tried to shake

off his grip again. "I cry every day and you've never once—"

"I cry," he said raggedly. He pressed the back of her hand to his wet cheek, so wrecked he didn't know how to deal with it except to work out harder, lose himself in books about her as a healthy, curious child. He compiled reports and translated documents and stalked her online. Anything so he didn't have to think about what they'd lost.

With a sob, she pivoted closer. Her other hand came up, feeling his cheek, finding the damp track running into his beard. She made a choking noise of surprise.

"It was such a miracle that she even happened." He could barely speak. His lungs were filled with acid. "It's like I'm being punished for what I've done to you, but it shouldn't have cost *her*. I keep thinking if I'd been there, maybe I could have done something—"

She pressed his face into her stomach. "I think those things, too. There wasn't."

He wrapped his arms around her and she cradled his head, and they shuddered under the grief that rocked them. They keened and shook and shared their anguish. After a time, she crumpled weakly into him.

He rolled her onto the mattress and they fit together like the complementary puzzle pieces they were, the way they always had.

"I don't want to make love. I just want you to hold me," she said between sniffles.

"I know. I will." He pulled the blankets across them and ironed her to his front, her damp face tucked against his aching throat, her sawing breaths cutting him in two.

He told her he was sorry. Sorry he wasn't there and sorry they'd lost her. She said, "Me, too," and pressed harder against him. "I could have lived without you if I had that connection, you know? I felt so alone after she was gone. Like you were really gone."

"Freja," he breathed, not telling her to shush as she sobbed piteously in his arms. And he didn't tell her he would be in her life forevermore because she wouldn't believe him.

But he would be. As he stroked her hair and eased her into sleep, he silently made her that promise. *I am here. I am yours. Always.*

Freja became aware of being too warm, yet incredibly comfortable, the way she used to feel when she slept with—

Her eyes were still gritty with last night's

tears as she dragged them open to see Giovanni's bearded throat.

He was awake, watching her through heavy lashes as his strong arms cradled her protectively. He was rock-hard against her stomach.

She quirked a brow at him. *Some things never change.*

His mouth dented at one corner with mild self-disgust. *Boys will be boys.*

The sweetest rush of affection suffused her. Something deeper, even, that she shied from acknowledging because she was still so gutted by hurt and betrayal. By the loss of *this*. Sometimes, when they'd had nothing between them but skin, she had believed in happily-ever-after. Then he had been gone. He had *left*. That's how it had felt, like an abandonment. She had felt so alone in these months without him, she could hardly face each day.

Last night had helped, though. It helped a lot to know she wasn't alone in her grief.

Last night's moment of need was over, though. She ought to roll away. Her defenses were still down and if she gave in to the compulsion to set her mouth against his skin and signal other needs, she would be in over her head again in no time.

"I can see you trying to make up your

mind," he said in a voice that held a morning rasp. "We'll take it slower this time."

His statement instantly infuriated her. "To where? Just because I'm thinking about sex, doesn't mean I want to stay married."

"Is that all you want?" A gruff laugh cut from his throat before his thick arms flexed to shift her against him, the subtle friction enough to bring every cell in her body to life. "Because you know I'm always up for that."

They were nose to nose and she could have given him a hard shove, but she kissed him. With aggression. Daring him to reject her. In fact, she threw her leg across him in a way that was pure muscle memory. Straddling him in the morning had been as routine as their shared breakfast and coffee.

He didn't roll onto his back to drag her atop him, though. He pressed her onto her back and loomed over her, one hand fondling her breast, teasing her nipple through lace as he kissed the hell out of her. His beard was surprisingly silky. An added sensation as he thrust his tongue between her lips so blatantly, she grew weak with yearning. A helpless noise throbbed in her throat.

He lifted his head and asked, "Is this really what you want?" His hand left her breast and gathered the short silk of her nightgown onto her stomach.

When he discovered she wasn't wearing underwear, he swore and thrust back the blankets.

"You've been naked under this all night?" he hissed in outrage.

"I always— *Ohh*."

He traced into her damp curls, parting her swollen folds, sending a rush of throbbing need through her whole body. She groaned and tried to close her legs against the intensity.

"Oh, no," he growled into her neck, using his body and his good thigh to keep her flat on the bed, legs open. "But be quiet or Marie will hear you."

He closed his mouth over her nipple and used his tongue to rub the rough lace of her nightgown against the swollen bud. At the same time, he eased two thick fingers into her slick channel.

"Giovanni," she hissed in acute pleasure, combing her fingers through his hair.

She played her hands over his shoulders, found his earlobes, made him bring his mouth to hers so they could kiss again, but as had often been the case, she was way ahead of him. Moments later, she wound up shattering, her cries of ecstasy muffled by his passionate kiss.

His touch grew tender, his kisses gentle. When she blinked open her eyes, his gray eyes were swirling like molten metal, turbulent with unsatisfied desire.

"Thank you. I needed that." His touch made a final circle of her damp, still sensitized flesh, sending a latent contraction through her. "I always want you, Freja. *Always*. Never doubt that. But I want more than this." He removed his hand and drew her nightgown down her thighs. "I want you to trust me with more than your body."

He had disarmed her so many times this way, leaving her trembling and pliant. This time she had to shake her head and say, "I don't know how I can."

"I know. That's why I thought we should wait for this." His rueful gaze went down her body and the tick of his cheek told her of the supreme control he was exercising over his urges. He dropped a last kiss on her mouth, one that had her parting her lips the way dry earth opened its pores to take in the rain after a drought.

When he pulled away, they were both breathing in unsteady pants.

"I'm going to shower. You'd best find your own across the hall." He sat up on the side of the bed, briefs straining to contain his rigid erection.

"Giovanni." Her hand impulsively went to his spine, where there were old scars from long-ago surgeries. "Thank you for last night. I needed *that*."

He caught her hand and twisted so he could press a kiss into her palm. For one second, she glimpsed a grief so profound, she wanted to pull him back into bed with her.

But he pulled away, transferring himself into his chair before he rolled into the bathroom.

She lay there a long time, hugging his pillow so she could breathe in his scent while she wondered if she really could do as he asked and trust him again.

Giovanni heard the helicopter as he was dressing.

He was still edgy with arousal and annoyed that they had to return to civilization so quickly. The original plan had been for Everett to quietly escort Freja to the SUV without any drama whatsoever. Giovanni had intended to whisk her quietly from the city and have as much time as they needed to reconcile before they were thrust into the spotlight again.

With Freja, however, one always had to expect the unexpected. That's why Giovanni had followed his intuition and said to the driver, "Pull around to the alley."

So Giovanni braced himself for just about anything as he moved into the lounge, finding only Everett at the island, sipping coffee. Marie was cooking. Freja was on the veranda, sitting at the small table that caught an hour of sunlight when beams angled into the valley, low and bright, first thing in the morning.

"Are Mummy and Daddy still fighting? Or have you kissed and made up?"

"You and I have had a good run, Everett. Don't ruin it by making me kill you." Giovanni smiled at Marie. "We'll eat outside with Freja."

"Freja is on a call with her intended," Everett supplied. "He wanted proof of life or he was going to provide these coordinates to anyone who would listen."

Giovanni shot him one dour look, then smoothly headed outside.

"—feel obliged to give it back," Nels was saying.

"You will not," Freja said firmly. "The financial side of our agreement stands. You'll still have a job, too." She flicked a defiant stare at Giovanni. "I won't stand for anything less considering the emotional distress you're enduring with the press right now."

"My concern is for you. You're definitely safe?"

"Completely. And I'll explain better once I'm back in New York. I'm really sorry for drawing you into this." Moments later, she ended the call and handed the device back to Everett, saying coolly to Giovanni, "I didn't have the skills to keep all that you've built from falling apart. Nels took it on in good faith and I expect you to reward him accordingly."

"About that. If he behaves himself and doesn't fight my retaking ownership, then yes, I will happily keep him on. But you and I are staying married until all the *i*'s are dotted and *t*'s crossed. If you want to divorce me after that, and sue me for more than what's in your prenup, that's fine, but I didn't amass this fortune by trusting blindly."

"No, it appears you built a lot of it by preying on other people's trust." She sent a critical glance at Everett and the house as she picked up her coffee and sipped.

"Giovanni assured me that you wouldn't expose our classified activities. Yesterday's video broke the internet so we have a lot of explaining ahead of us. Can we count on you?"

"I don't know. Let me check with my handlers in Pyongyang."

"Bidduzza." Giovanni took her hand and gave it an admonishing squeeze. "How many people did you tell that you believed I was alive?"

"Just Nels. And I only asked if he thought it was worth my hiring a private investigator to look into whether you could be alive, since I'd been given ashes and a death certificate, but hadn't seen your body. He said I was having trouble accepting my loss."

"Did you tell him or anyone else that the ring had been stolen?"

"No. They would have said I misplaced it since the rest of the jewelry was still there. But it made me wonder *why* you'd gone into hiding. For instance, if you were in financial trouble, you would have stolen the jewels to square off with your creditors. If you were being chased by the law, you would have made a better effort to take money with you, not leave so much to me."

She glanced at the house again, perhaps rightly deducing that he had as much money off the books as he did on. He had plans to donate this and other properties like it to amputees and other charities. He wasn't a tax dodger, but he could clarify that another time.

"It felt a lot like you were hiding from *me*, especially after we had that awful fight, but it seemed a pretty drastic way to end things." The line of her mouth wavered and her brow crinkled. "The most logical conclusion was that you disappeared to protect your life, in which case it made sense to act as though I believed you were dead. Getting engaged seemed to reinforce that illusion and since Nels was willing to take over your business interests and I happen to trust him, he made a good choice."

Giovanni had taken one look at the engagement announcement and had nearly thrown himself off this veranda. Not once had it occurred to him that she'd done it out of concern for him.

"Also, I thought if I made this production of a marriage, you would either show up or you wouldn't." Her mouth pursed in dismay. "At least I would know where we stood."

"And I'm the fool for thinking she had the capacity to be an operative?" Everett scoffed. "Freja, darling, how would you like an extremely well-paying career that provides ample opportunity for travel? Because I know people who would love to meet you."

"Don't. You. Dare," Giovanni said from between his teeth.

"But she could be so helpful when she goes back to North Korea," Everett said. "Does he know you've been looking into that?"

Giovanni's heart stopped. "No, he does not know that. What the *hell*, Freja?"

"You're worried about whether *you* can trust *me*?" she asked Everett, splaying an outraged hand on her chest.

"I'm going to get more coffee." Everett rose. "Nels is gay, by the way." He patted Giovanni's shoulder. "Deep in the closet, but super gay."

"What a horrible person! I know it was you who stole the ring. I can tell by your cologne," she called to Everett's retreating back, looking at the chair he'd vacated and left askew. "And the fact you didn't push the chair in at the desk."

Everett was gone and she sat back with a disgruntled look.

"Are you out of your mind? You're not going back to North Korea." Giovanni's riches could accomplish many things, but he doubted he could get her out of there again. Not without costs that were higher than monetary ones. "Just because you were treated well the first time does not mean they would roll out the red carpet if you returned. For God's sake, Freja! At *best* you'd wind up in a work camp."

"I didn't have you, I didn't have our baby. Sung-mi and Byung-woo are the only family I have left. Don't judge me for wanting to see them."

"I don't. But you have me now."

She flinched and looked to the far side of the valley, profile troubled.

Time, he thought with frustration. They had never had it, they needed it now, and he didn't want to wait. He wanted everything put right between them. Now.

"Everett might be able to call in some favors and make some inquiries. He's worth having on your side."

"Are you trying to bribe me to keep my mouth shut? I won't say a thing about you and your dumb spy games. You don't have to threaten Sung-mi and Nels, either."

"That's not what this is."

"Sure," she said flatly, clearly disbelieving him, but Everett came back and they talked about what they would say at the press conference.

Freja didn't bother packing. She had clothes in all of Giovanni's residences including the penthouse in Rome, which was where they went.

All his residential staff had been instructed to close up and go down to skeletal once she'd gone back to New York. It had felt so strange to return to America. She hadn't been away that long, but she'd been a completely different person and was again as they returned to the last place they'd been together. She saw everything with fresh eyes.

The place had been kept up, of course. The plants were healthy and there wasn't a speck of dust anywhere. The housekeeper was busy restocking the kitchen, smiling cheerfully, though wide-eyed with astonishment that her employer was alive.

But the top-level security and tinted windows and soundproof doors weren't just protecting Giovanni's wealth or privacy, Freja realized now. The quick escape routes via helicopter or the manually controlled service elevator weren't just for fire safety.

Giovanni made a call to his barber, who appeared with a flush on his cheeks as though he'd run the whole way.

While they disappeared to make him presentable, she dug into her closet for one of her couture day dresses, choosing a three-quarter-length shirtdress. Its navy color was brightened by small white polka dots and a crisp white collar and cuffs. She kept the look simple, using a straightening iron on her hair before tying it back with a navy ribbon. She finished her light makeup with a soft pink gloss.

When she returned to the lounge, Everett was there, nursing a drink.

"I thought you were talking with Giovanni," she said, trying to explain away her dismayed double take when she saw him.

"No need. He and I have always been on the same page—for the most part." He sipped, watching her over his glass. "Were you on your way out?"

"No." Had she thought about it? Absolutely. Giovanni had been right when he had said they had a habit of running too fast. Too hot. Too hard. The way she had burst into flames under his touch this morning was completely typical.

The temptation to let that familiar urgency sweep her up and carry her away was strong, but she didn't know if she dared set herself up for another heartbreak, not after the first one had nearly destroyed her. She definitely didn't know how to trust that it wouldn't happen again.

"No?" Everett needled, as if he read all her misgivings clear as a neon sign. As if her desire to stay or go was any of his business.

"Is that why you're sitting here?" she asked crossly, making an unnecessary adjustment to a throw that was already draped perfectly over the back of the sofa. "Are you guarding me in case I decide to bolt?"

"Yes."

His frankness startled her, but she only muttered, "Well, isn't that just like Giovanni to ask for my trust, but not offer any in return."

"He didn't ask me to do this. I thought of it all by myself."

"The nineties called. They said the cold war is over and the KGB is a pop band now."

"I'm starting to see the attraction." Everett drained his glass and set it aside. "Giovanni is a man of principle and duty and tremendous loyalty, so he did everything he could to honor the commitments he had made to the job we were doing, but from the moment he met you, his priorities were impacted. I didn't understand it, but I knew from your first night together that I was losing him to you."

"So you stole him back? How mean-girl of you." She clasped her elbows as she moved to the windows and looked out on the view across the rooftops to the Colosseum and the Roman Forum.

"If only it was that easy. I genuinely thought you might have had something to do with that explosion. He was beside himself, though. If he hadn't been in traction, he would have crawled out of the hospital to go to you. The stubborn bastard wouldn't even speak to me until I got that ring back onto his finger. The only reason he stayed in hiding was for *your* safety. When I had to tell him you'd lost the baby… Let's just say it was a very bad day."

"And yet he didn't come," she said with lingering anguish tightening her throat.

"Has he told you anything of what we've been doing?" Impatience edged into his tone.

"He told me it was more important than I am." She clung to her sharp elbows. "Maybe it was. It doesn't make any of these lies easier to bear."

"So you're going to punish him for it? Leave him because of it? You'll destroy him, Freja. You have that power. Do you understand that? Your engagement to Nels—"

"Everett." Giovanni spoke in a quiet voice that was so lethal, Freja's heart clunked with alarm in her chest.

His clean shave and fresh haircut left Giovanni so imperially handsome, a stab of emotion hit her eyes. Attraction soared into her blood along with joy at his mere existence here and pride that such a gorgeous man could be called hers. Her *husband*.

If she dared to give him another chance.

"You are no longer part of this marriage," he said to Everett. "Never interfere between me and Freja again. Do you understand?"

Everett threw up his hands. "I'll be gone after the press conference."

How long would *she* be here? That was the decision she had to make, Freja realized with a pang of distress.

"You look lovely," Giovanni said with an appreciative slip of his gaze down to her navy pumps and back. "Perfect."

"You look nice, too," she murmured, still experiencing the pull of physical allure he always exerted over her. "Are we holding it downstairs? Or…?"

"Yes. My collar is wet so I'll change my shirt." He spoke in a distracted tone, rolling forward as he did. He picked up one of the hands she was trying to untangle from the other. "Where is your wedding band?"

"New York. This was in the safe and seemed a better choice than the engagement ring. It's your mother's anniversary ring."

"I know." He turned the white-gold eternity band encrusted with baguette-cut diamonds.

"If you don't want me to wear it—"

"I do. It's a good choice. Thank you."

His gaze was a depthless quicksilver pool that she could have fallen into, but Everett cleared his throat.

"The sooner we do our thing, the sooner I'll be gone."

Giovanni's mouth twitched wryly. He dropped his hands to his wheels.

"Giovanni," she said, forcing him to pivot to face her. She drew a breath that burned like the arid winds off a million miles of desert, but a bubble of something big and optimistic filled her throat. "I'm glad you're alive."

CHAPTER EIGHT

FREJA STOOD AMID the blinding camera lights and flashes, one hand on Giovanni's shoulder as he and Everett balanced on the razor's edge between truth and fabrication, never mentioning their extracurricular activities. They claimed Freja's very public engagement had been a ruse to support Giovanni's supposed "accident" and passed off these horrendous few months as an elaborate plan by an eccentric billionaire to thwart a death threat while the culprits were hunted down.

Thankfully, it was over quickly. Everett took his leave and Freja didn't realize Giovanni had pushed the button for the rooftop until the doors opened at the helicopter pad.

"We're not staying here? This is just like you, springing a flight on me out of the blue!" She gave a frantic wave of her hand. "Nothing in our calendar, just, 'Get in and shut up.' You're worse than my father when it comes to moving along on the spur of the moment. At least he gave me time to *pack*."

"Everett had your things retrieved from Milan." Giovanni pointed to her distinctive, monogrammed luggage going into the cargo area. "And I just said in the press conference that we would be spending time at home for the next week or two. Where do you think my home is, Freja?"

"I don't know! You have a dozen of them."

"Sicily." He was taking a tone as if all of this was obvious. "We're going to my villa on my family estate. I can't leave the country until Everett has me sufficiently resuscitated for bureaucrats to issue a new passport."

"Oh. I knew there was a villa there. I didn't know you thought of it as 'home.' Why didn't you take me there before?"

"I was working," he said with his *don't ask* shuttered expression that always hit her with the force of a wrecking ball.

Her heart shrank and her skin grew too tight as she climbed aboard and buckled in.

Giovanni came in and anchored his chair, releasing a frustrated sigh as he did. "There are things I will never be able to talk about, Freja. You will have to accept that."

She tried to shake it off with a small shrug, keeping her profile turned to the window.

They were served a light meal as they flew. She choked it down, but the pilaf tasted like glue and the silence stuck in her ears.

They landed behind a villa that sprawled atop a hillock overlooking a sweeping slope to the sea. Everything was bathed in a fading mauve light while the setting sun painted a red line against the horizon.

"This is beautiful," she couldn't help saying as they moved along a paved path flanked by shrubs strung with fairy lights. The air was balmy and feather-soft, flavored by the mature orange grove and the earthy scents of the surrounding vineyards. "The house looks quite new, though."

"It is." He veered down a paved path to a bricked area surrounding the pool. Quite a ways down the slope, off to the left, stood a shoe-shaped house. Its gray stones were lit by floodlights buried within its surrounding gardens. "That's where I was born. Where we would come in the summer and Christmas, when my father wasn't dragging us elsewhere for work. It's regarded as a heritage site so I couldn't remodel it to accommodate my chair, not without destroying its character."

"That's—" Incredibly sad. She'd always envied people who knew where their home was, but to be able to see it and not be able to enter? "It looks occupied."

"Staff use it." He pivoted and leaned into pushing himself up an incline that skirted the pool's blue glow, leading her to an open double-door entrance.

His housekeeper greeted him with teary warmth and welcomed Freja with belated congratulations on their marriage. Since they'd just eaten, they said they would dine later, after they'd had time to settle in and relax.

Like all of Giovanni's homes, this one was scrupulously tailored to his chair, with a full contingent of people ready to look after his every need. The decor was simple and soothing and sumptuously comfortable, encouraging relaxation. The huge estate was fenced and security patrolled, he informed her when she expressed concern for the open doors.

"This isn't New York. The cat burglars are actual cats from the vineyard looking for a morsel or a scratch between the ears."

Her suitcases were already in the master

bedroom when they got there, but there was a small selection of clothing in the closet, too.

"I've never seen these," she murmured as she fingered through bohemian skirts and sleeveless knit tops. "When did you order them?"

"Sent from Milan after one of your initial fittings, I imagine. I expected we would make it here eventually."

"They're so casual." Comfortable and relaxing.

"Even when I have social commitments here, they're low-key events. We dress down for dinner." He showed her the shorts and collared T-shirt he retrieved from a drawer.

The tension that had been gripping her for ages began to release. She stepped out of her spiked pumps and tugged a crinkled cotton peasant dress from a hanger.

"I thought you might have come here after..." He didn't finish, but she knew he was referring to his own funeral. "Why did you go back to New York? Why did you buy your own place there?"

Because she hadn't been able to face any reminders of him.

"So many people were asking about the business. It seemed more convenient to be there, especially once I asked Nels for help. He wanted to include me in the decisions he was making. And this… Your life, being your wife. It seemed like it hadn't really happened. I hadn't been Signora Catalano long enough to know how to pull it off. It was easier to go back to where I'd put my life on track twice before."

But had she? Oliver's townhome hadn't been her life. Nor had university. Haring off to Europe with Giovanni hadn't offered the sort of stability and purpose she had longed for. What sort of life did she even want to pursue?

"We could make this our home from now on. I'll still have travel demands, but not nearly so many." He followed her out of the closet.

She sat down on the end of the bed, crumpling the dress onto her knees, lips parted as she tried to think of how to respond.

"Don't say you don't want that," he commanded gruffly. Maybe it was a plea. His voice was low and held strain, as though he was speaking while having a bullet removed from his chest. "We could try again for a family, Freja."

With a small sob of longing, she hugged the formless dress to her stomach.

She did want that. A baby. Children. She knew that now. She wanted a family. People who were hers.

She didn't realize she had closed her eyes until his hand touched her knee and she blinked her lids open.

"Did the doctors say anything about… Are there concerns about future pregnancies?" he asked apprehensively. "I don't want to put you through that if—"

"No." She bit her lips together. She had asked those questions herself and found cold comfort in the answers. "They didn't identify any serious health issue and said my chances of a successful pregnancy next time were exactly the same as any other woman's."

He nodded in distant understanding, hand caressing her knee. "That's something to think about, then. Isn't it? Trying again, when we're ready?"

She didn't need to think about it. She knew that much with unshaken certainty deep in her core. Pushing the dress off her lap, she scooted backward onto the bed.

"Can we try right now?"

"Freja." He closed his eyes, expression twisting with agony. "We need *time*."

"I need *hope*," she argued raggedly. "I need to feel something that isn't emptiness and agony and self-doubt."

"*Tisoru*, you know that's all this would be. Hope." His voice was tortured, his hands in fists on his thighs. "A thin one! I can't make it happen every time. You know that. If you're sure about wanting a family, then let's do this properly. We'll renew our vows and see a specialist and find a way. It will be a journey we take with intention, together, every step of the way."

"A chance is enough for now." Was it? Not really, but, "If it's meant to be, if *we* are meant to be, like you said yesterday, then it will happen for us again."

"Don't do that, Freja." His expression turned grave. "That is far too much pressure to put on a relationship as fragile as ours is right now. Don't do that to us."

"I need something, Giovanni! A sign. A message from the universe to convince me that I should stay with you, because my head is telling me I should be in New York by now, forgetting I ever knew you."

His breath hissed and he swore at the ceiling.

"This morning used up my lifetime's allotment of good intentions." He threw away the clothes in his lap and his biceps flexed as he joined her on the bed. "If you want to make love, I will make love with you. *Always.* But understand that I view this as a resumption of our marriage. You will not get rid of me so easily next time."

"I didn't get rid of you the first time, you idiot!"

"Call me names if you have to." He dragged himself to loom over her. "Pinch and bite me. Get all that anger out because I don't want it between us anymore."

"You put it there! You did this."

"I did." He sounded gruff, his good leg was crushing her thigh, but his lips were tantalizingly sweet as he pressed airy kisses along her jawline.

"You said I was overreacting. That I was smothering you and acting like a jealous shrew."

"I did." He set those tender kisses over her eyes, closing them, and rubbed his lips against her brow. "I was worried. I wanted you away from me, off the street so no one would guess who you were. And you tried to protect me afterward anyway. I don't deserve you, Freja. I know that."

So many soft, soft kisses that stirred more than sensual excitement. They crept close to the heart she'd been guarding so very carefully since the beginning. Oh, she had been falling in love as fast as she'd fallen into bed with him. Too fast even to recognize what was happening and put words to it. Then they had been married and all the small secrets began piling up, eating at her, causing her to hold back her tenuous new feelings.

She had fought and fought and fought not to love him, but stunted as his disappearance had left her emotionally, she had continued to yearn for him. For the only man who made her heart lift and race.

She loved him. She had known that when she chased him to Dubrovnik, desperate to know where they stood.

She was still desperate, wanting to fill herself with him. She skated her hands across the ripple of his muscled chest and drank in the rumbling hum of his pleasured noise.

His lips seductively touched one corner of her mouth then the other, finally giving her a tiny peck that was nowhere near enough.

"Why do you always tease?" she scolded,

cupping the side of his smooth cheek and urging him to kiss her properly.

He did. Slow and thorough until she moaned in the agonized ecstasy of having him here with her. But for how long this time?

"I'm not teasing, *bidduzza*. I'm savoring." He released the first button on her dress and kissed the inch of breastbone he exposed. "I'm reacquainting myself the way I should have this morning. Why are you always in such a hurry? We have time."

"Do we?" she asked baldly. "Because I have never believed that."

He frowned.

"You only married me because I was pregnant. You were shutting me out. I thought you resented me."

"Ah, Freja. No." He rested his forehead against her chin.

On that fateful last day, she'd asked him, *Do you love me? Do you even want to be married?* She couldn't bear to ask it again, fearful of how he would respond.

"I didn't see how we could last when things were so tense and awful," she admitted painfully. "When you were disappearing and keeping secrets. I followed you that day to end the suspense of *when*."

He made a noise of defeat.

"I wanted *that* to be over so I could be here." He slipped another button free. "I won't shut you out again." His lips went down as he opened more and more of her dress. "We have time. I promise you."

She wanted to believe him. She did.

His hand slid beneath the edge of her dress and cupped her bare breast. She gasped, arching as he plumped the swell, exposing it to his pleased gaze.

"My beautiful rebel," he said with affection for her braless state. He dipped his head and sucked her nipple.

How many times had she dreamed of this? Imagined him in the bed beside her, making love with her again.

"I missed you," she confessed in a whisper and ran her hands into his hair, savoring him, too. Because they might last or they might not, but she had him now and she wanted to love him with every part of her.

Everything slowed then. Each caress was drawn out, each kiss achingly tender. Each layer of clothing peeled away bit by bit until they were naked with nothing between them but desire that scorched their skin as they moved against one another.

He spoke to her in his beautiful language, kissing every inch of her until she was weak with longing. She did the same, holding back her pleasure so they would experience it together when she was sprawled upon him, taking him in. Joined with him again in the most intimate way. Finally.

In this moment she believed, as she always had, that they were anointed by ancient gods. There was nothing more sacred than the feel of him inside her, their rocking as universal as the waves rolling up the sands of a beach and the sway of trees in the wind.

But this union was only a stolen moment from time. A gift and a curse because eventually the crisis hit and even though it was magnificent, it marked the end.

And even though she was sated and bursting with love for him, and even though he cradled her in his arms as they caught their breath, she felt them slide apart and had to press her eyes closed against hot tears.

"You have to love the modern news cycle," Freja said over breakfast the next morning. "Your return from the dead has already been overshadowed by a golf club that has finally allowed women to join, a bitcoin embezzlement, and a kitten rescued from a ledge on a skyscraper."

"How do I compete with such a hero?" Giovanni lifted his head from the market numbers he was studying on his tablet. "Surely I'm more photogenic than a window washer?"

"He was a firefighter and any man's appearance improves tenfold when he holds a kitten or a puppy. It's a proven social media fact. Ugh," she added with a dismayed flick through her feed. "Trolls are saying your faked death was a stunt to sell more of my books."

"Ignore them," Giovanni insisted. "Turn that off. I want to show you the estate."

"I have to answer a few emails first. The publicity team for my book is having a bird that I didn't warn them about any of this." Freja frowned. "*Tsk*. And even though my first book isn't out yet, I'm being asked for a follow-up. A tell-all about our marriage. No, thank you." She swiped dismissively, but her tablet continued to ping. "This is ridiculous. Are you being inundated with invitations to charity galas and holiday mixers? I don't even know most of these people."

"The advantages of a new phone. I'm sure

they'll find me in due course." He had had a mind to skip reentering the social whirl in favor of a honeymoon, but he'd forgotten about her book tour. "I'll make some calls today, begin the search for a new team of assistants. The most inconvenient consequence of pretending to be dead has to be the loss of so many well-trained staff."

"That'll teach you. Don't do it again," she said dourly.

Amusement tugged at the corners of his mouth. "When are we due in New York for the book launch?"

"November first. Will you be alive by then? You don't have to come."

"Of course I'll be there. Do we factor in a visit to Paris on the way? Surely you need a new wardrobe for it?"

"Does anyone 'need' a new wardrobe for anything?" She kept her chin tucked as she lifted her lashes to send a scathing glance at him. Her gaze dropped to the screen and her nose wrinkled. "I'm not even sure how many appearances I'll have. I managed to cancel most of my interviews when you disappeared. Now that I'm not actually a widow, I'm being asked to reinstate them and do more. I'll try to keep it to a minimum."

"My calendar is your calendar. Enjoy your moment in the sun."

"I burn easily," she dismissed.

He had missed this. So much his chest felt strained, trying to contain the bubble of lightness inside him. He had missed her facetious asides in that honeyed voice, her white-blond brows that pulled together in concentration, and the fine, angel-blond strands of hair that lifted with static, begging his hand to reach across and smooth them flat.

She looked up when he did, then rolled her eyes and dampened her palm with the condensation on her juice glass to flatten the flyaway strands herself.

He bit back a chuckle, unable to think of a time when he'd felt so content.

Lovemaking after a dry spell had that effect on a man, he supposed.

He sobered as he acknowledged it was so much more than that. Sex with Freja was as exquisite as ever and he was enormously gratified to be intimate with her again, but he was worried about the expectation she was placing on them. He wasn't even sure if bringing a baby into this relationship while they were still finding their way was the best thing.

Not that he could say so. It would break

these fragile threads of connection they were weaving between them with the return to physical closeness. That's why he'd given in—aside from the sheer pleasure in the act. He knew his limitations and the chance of another natural conception was extremely low, but the intimacy of lovemaking would begin laying the foundation of trust they desperately needed.

He brought her hand to his mouth so he could kiss her palm.

"What was that for?" she asked, blue eyes dazzled, mouth tilting into a pleased smile.

"You're beautiful." It was the simple truth. Gazing on her, he felt physical pain at how incredibly lovely she was. At how much it meant to him to have her in his life again.

Her gaze softened to an intense vulnerability, the kind that threw a tremendous weight of responsibility onto him, one of such magnitude, he didn't know how to live up to it. He had wanted to rise to it, though. That's what had taken him to Dubrovnik.

He had been hurrying toward his wife and child and a shimmering possibility that went beyond the buoyant joy of orgasms and banter and *I'm glad you're alive*. It was deep and wide and so powerful, it could destroy him if he let it. If he embraced it and lost again.

His inner walls shook, but fear clenched icy fingers around him. Fear of yet another loss. He took an emotional step back even as she dampened her lips and her mouth trembled as though she was about to say something. As though she waited for him to say something.

"I say yes to Paris. You deserve to mark your accomplishment with something special," he said.

It was a mistake. He knew it immediately, even before the light had died from her expression. The thing he feared losing was gone.

"I'll think about it." She rose and offered a smile that didn't reach her eyes. "Let me make my calls, and then you can show me the estate." She walked away.

Freja's first pregnancy had been a complete fluke. Logically, she knew it wasn't fair to hinge their reconciliation on something so capricious as another miracle, but even though everything had changed between her and Giovanni, nothing had.

Oh, he had time for her now. In that way things were as magical as their first days together. They swam and toured his estate on an all-terrain tractor fitted for him to operate with his hands. He had a topless Jeep that was also tricked out with a hydraulic ramp so he could drive it while sitting in his wheelchair. He stayed out of the busy city centers, but toured her along the coast, and they stopped to window-shop in small villages and ordered espresso and biscotti at outdoor cafés.

He even took her inland to Piazza Armerina, the town where her father had wandered an ancient Roman complex for a week while Freja learned fencing in a grassy park.

"The infamous bikini girls," Giovanni said when she suggested he turn that direction, referring to the famed mosaics in the ruins. "I was taken there on a school outing. My extremely high expectations were left unmet."

She chuckled. "I liked the circus pictures and all the strange creatures, but my attention span was exhausted within the hour. Thus, the fencing lessons."

"I read all those books of your father's yet never quite understood what drove him to pursue such a vagabond life. It was his living, obviously, but my father traveled for work and I still knew where I was from. I had a home to come back to."

A tendril of her hair had escaped from

her ponytail and caught at the corner of her mouth. She dragged it away as she said, "Yeah, but if you never have a home, you'll never be homesick."

"Is that true?" The car geared down with a small growl as he slowed for traffic. He glanced at her. "Are you missing America now that you've made a home there?"

"I miss Sung-mi and Byung-woo," she said with a crooked, *What can you do?* smile. "I kept waiting for New York to feel like home, but I actually felt more in my natural habitat when I was traveling with you, waking up in a new city every other day. Granted, you travel very comfortably," she allowed dryly. Private jets and luggage handlers made all the difference. "But even though your unannounced itinerary changes were really annoying—you do need to work on your communication skills—being on the move feels very normal to me."

"I don't want that life for either of us anymore. I want you to feel like this is your home."

She had pieced that together over these days of his proudly showing her every inch of this admittedly beautiful and ever-changing island.

"Is that unrealistic?" he asked in a guarded voice.

"I don't know." Part of her was thinking, *Home is where the heart is.* That's why she'd been content moving around with her father and living in a type of lockdown with Sung-mi.

By that logic, all she should need was Giovanni, but her heart was pining.

Because he didn't love her the way those people had. And if he wasn't willing to open his heart to her, then she didn't have a home with him.

CHAPTER NINE

GIOVANNI WAS READING through CVs from his headhunter when Freja walked into his study. Rather than the beach bum attire they'd both fallen into while here, she wore jeans, a pale gray top and a light blazer with pockets—the sort of clothes she wore for travel.

"I thought we decided to stay in for dinner." They'd only finished their late lunch an hour ago. "You look pale," he noted. "What's wrong?"

"I—" She closed the door.

He clicked off the tablet, met her by the chair where she sank down and tried to wrest the fingers of her one hand off the other. She wasn't wearing his mother's ring or any other.

Everything in him stilled.

"I've decided to go back to New York. There's a flight from Palermo in a couple of hours."

"Something with the tour? Everett will be here with my passport tomorrow. We were going to stop in Paris."

"I don't—" She shook her head and said in a small voice, "I'm not pregnant."

The words rang through him like a sonic boom, leveling everything inside him. He firmly set aside whatever emotions rose up in waves around that news and said, "We both know my limitations."

The timing was wrong, too. He was no fertility expert, but he understood the basics and they'd only started having sex a week ago.

"Freja." He reached out to still her twisting hands. "There's no rush. We have time to try again, find ways to tip the odds in our favor."

"I thought if I got pregnant again, it would mean our marriage is worth continuing." She stood up and paced anxiously across the room.

While he fell back in his chair and fought to keep panic from overwhelming him, he did what he had always done in times of heightened stakes and deep emotion. He condensed all of it into a ball deep in his core, stomach tight as he forced himself to ignore it so he could think past it.

"I told you that we shouldn't put that sort of

pressure on us," he said forcefully enough to make her stiffen. He softened his tone. "We can see what happens for now, try more seriously later."

"What if it doesn't happen? What if that's the only reason we stay married and it doesn't happen?" she asked with a little sob of despair. "Think about it. You dated me to investigate me. You married me because I was pregnant. You told me we had to stay married until you took control of your company. Tomorrow you get your passport and can resume your life. And you want to share it with me? Try for a baby?"

"Wanting a family is a good reason to stay married."

"But if it doesn't happen, what do we have? We were never suited. Isn't it better to end it now? Don't you want to marry someone you love and have a real family?"

"For God's sake, Freja. You're not even giving us a chance." He had to hold on to that cold, angry tone or the agony would shatter the steel walls holding his emotions inside. "This is not fair. I can't make that happen on demand. *You know that.*"

"This isn't about your physical limitations! It's about your emotional ones. I asked you months ago if you loved me. You still haven't answered me."

Because death had bled love out of him once and losing their baby had done it again. He had been trying to keep what they had to something he could manage. Something that didn't have the potential to destroy them both.

And what if he *couldn't* give her a baby? He couldn't bear to put her through the anguish of that. Or of losing another pregnancy. He'd already put her through *so much*.

"I think this is for the best," she said, voice papery in the silence. "I'm going to go."

He had to let her. Didn't he?

"Have you lost your mind?" Everett said when Giovanni told him Freja had left for America last night. "You went through all of this and you *let her go*?"

"News flash. Women are no longer chattel. They do what they want. And I put her through the wringer. She'd had enough."

"Is that what she said?"

"No."

"What then?"

"None of your business. I told you to butt out."

"You're always so surly when you haven't

slept." Everett moved to help himself to a scotch even though it wasn't even noon yet. "Are you coming back to work for me, then?"

"No."

"No?" Everett turned with a knowing smirk. "Why not?"

"Oh, shut up. I had to wait for my passport." He dropped it into the satchel hanging off his chair, the one that already held his phone, tablet, and wheelchair repair tools. His private jet was fueled and ready when he was. "I thought about having her dragged off the plane, but..."

He had hoped she would change her mind. So he could stay exactly as closed off as he was. So he would know she loved him before he had to confess to it first.

He pinched the bridge of his nose. "What happens if I tell her I love her? What changes? Nothing. I'm still me. Still in this chair. Still dragging her around the world to attend board meetings or whatever bloody thing comes up. She wants a baby and so do I, but there's no guarantee with things like that. Failure is hell. So what do I offer her that isn't...a promise of pain?"

This was what had kept him awake all night. Despair. A complete lack of hope. He couldn't give her happily-ever-after. There was no such thing.

"I've been told to butt out," Everett said laconically. "But what do you want from her? Because she's pretty and all, but she's just a woman. She's not offering you any guarantees that she can produce an heir, is she? Or never wind up ill or needing a chair? Find someone else."

"How obtuse are you?" Giovanni asked with affront. "I don't *want* anyone else. She doesn't have to *give* me anything. I just want her here, in my life. Then all the pains and disappointments of existence are bearable at least."

"Again, I don't want to overstep," Everett said, scratching his upper lip and serving up his remark with buckets of irony. "But is there *any* chance she feels the same?"

Giovanni wanted to say something biting, but a ray of sunshine peeked through the thick walls inside him, throwing light into the darkness even as its heat touched on raw places and stung.

It was painful, but it tugged him to take one more chance.

"Make yourself at home. I'm leaving."

* * *

Freja was missing Giovanni even before she got on the plane to New York. She sat down next to a man who snored the whole way and tried to hold back her tears.

She reminded herself he didn't love her. Leaving was the smart thing to do, before they were too entangled for her to leave this easily again.

That's what she told Nels when he picked her up at the airport and asked, "What happened?"

He took her back to the apartment she'd bought and told him to use because he was being hounded by the press. They shared a bottle of wine and she fed him the lines about the death threat, keeping Giovanni's secret, but she apologized to Nels for using him.

"I was using you, too. But… I have to say it. You can have the man you want, Freja. I can't. So why are you squandering that?"

She didn't have a good answer. Fear? She had never let that hold her back. Distrust? She understood and accepted why Giovanni had hurt her. The only way to find out if he would do it in the future was to give him another chance.

Her brain went around in circles and, in a

desperate bid for distraction, she agreed to do a reading from an advance copy of her book. Her agent found a bookstore willing to throw it together at the last minute. They put up a few posters and she mentioned it on her social media accounts, but it was so low-key, she didn't even dress up for it. She wore brown plaid pants with ankle boots and a sage-green pullover with sleeves that fell to her knuckles.

She begged Nels to come with her, certain no one would show up, swearing, "I'm fine with talking to an empty room. This is a test drive for the other appearances I have lined up, but I'd like some feedback."

The shop was in one of Greenwich Village's character buildings, the kind that had been through a thousand iterations and would go through a thousand more in service to the changing demographics of the foot traffic that passed it. Presently it catered to the pseudo-intellectuals who appreciated the reclaimed floorboards and fair-trade coffee and the reading area in the loft that offered free Wi-Fi.

The overstuffed furniture in that loft had been pushed to the rail and a dozen chairs brought in. They were already full when Freja arrived and the harried staff were frantically stealing stools from the coffee bar and carrying chairs from someone's office. A queue had started on the stairs that ran all the way out the door.

"Those people aren't all here for me," Freja said to Nels, pointing out, "They're all holding my father's books."

"Still a nice show of support."

"It is." She forced a smile, thinking her publishing team would love that it was turning into a standing-room-only event. She knew this should feel like a triumph of some kind, but even though Nels stayed nearby, she felt very...lonely.

They moved her a little closer to the rail so the people on the stairs could see her, and they introduced her.

Freja smiled at the crowd and began to read her own words:

"'Some people view life as a battle or an adventure, one where you fight to overcome adversity in hopes of a thrilling victory. Some see it as a garden, where you weed out what doesn't work and nurture what does. They tell you to stop to smell the roses.'"

There was a small ripple of laughter, thank goodness.

"'My father saw life as a journey. Traveling was his life and thus it was mine, but I always saw myself as a passenger. I didn't get to decide where we were going, but I didn't mind. When you're with someone you love, it doesn't matter where you're going or how long it takes to get there.'"

She faltered slightly, having forgotten she had written that. She cleared her throat and continued.

"'Pappa was my constant, even though the rest of the relationships in my life were transitory. When he died so unexpectedly, I was devastated, but there was a piece of me that accepted the loss as normal. No one is permanent. Eventually, you have to say goodbye to everyone.'"

Did she, though? It was striking her that she had done this. She had pushed Giovanni away. That's why she had gone to Dubrovnik that day, to say goodbye. She hadn't believed there was such a thing as building a life together. Yes, there had been things between them that had to be overcome, but it wasn't all on him to convince her they had a future. She could make that choice and pursue it herself.

"'So I knew...'" Her voice was wavering in and out as emotion overwhelmed her. "'I knew in my heart of hearts...'"

She began to shake. She couldn't do this. Why had she let him go? She wanted to go to him right now. *When you're with someone you love…*

"Freja." Nels touched her arm and nodded to the floor below.

Giovanni blocked the aisle between stacks of books. He hadn't shaved and his hair was ruffled. He was never a man to wear his heart on his sleeve, but as everyone craned their necks to see where her attention had gone, he had eyes only for her. He touched his fingertips to his mouth and blew her a kiss.

The whole crowd sighed.

She released a teary laugh.

"I'll go down," Nels whispered, squeezing her arm. "You can do this."

"I didn't expect my husband to be here." She sniffed back her tears and took a deep breath and pulled it together. "But I'm so glad he is."

She set her fingertip under her own words and picked up where she had left off.

"'I knew in my heart of hearts that I would not be in North Korea forever. That my journey would continue eventually…'"

Freja was tied up for hours. While she read, the place was so silent, the couple of times the barista caused the espresso machine to hiss, the poor woman earned a dozen dirty looks.

After a lengthy round of applause, people wanted selfies and her autograph in her father's books.

"I'm so sorry," she said when the crowd finally thinned out and she was able to come down to Giovanni.

"Why? You were working. Your fiancé kept me company."

Nels went red and started to stammer. "Freja and I have talked and we're not—"

"That was a joke," Giovanni assured him and offered his card. "Call me tomorrow. We'll talk properly about the handoff, which will still be very much hands-on."

Giovanni was already thinking he wanted as much time as possible with Freja and, judging by tonight, she had commitments of her own.

"You were spectacular," he told her as Nels left them alone.

She brushed off the compliment with a flushed smile. It faded slightly as she asked, "Why are you here?"

"To see you. Can I buy you dinner?"

"I'm not hungry. I could use a stiff drink, though," she joked.

"There's champagne at the apartment."

"You want me to come home with you?" She dipped her chin, pleased and not at all as surprised as she was pretending.

"I do. Right now."

Freja took a few calls in the car and apologized again as they entered the penthouse.

"*Bidduzza*, you have been very tolerant of my work. I'm happy to support yours. In fact, I'm so proud, my shirt shouldn't have any buttons left."

"Even though I left Sicily the way I did? I've had time to think, you know." Time to regret leaving so abruptly.

"Come here. I want to tell you something." He rolled closer to the sofa and moved onto it.

She followed and sank down next to him. He angled toward her and took her hand.

"Stefano and I were only thirteen months apart. Because of that, we did almost everything together, but when he turned fifteen, he was allowed to get a real job. It was a summer student position and he swore it was no better than glorified babysitting, but he was not at home weeding the vineyard to earn his allowance the way I was. The envy I felt that summer nearly ate me alive. I was excited for the next year when I presumed we would teach fencing together."

She saw the shadows closing in on his gray eyes and swallowed. His thumb moved restlessly across the backs of her knuckles.

"He took after our mother. She was exuberant like him. Quite playful and funny. He got her black, curly hair and pointy chin. I have our father's eyes and jaw. Papà was a more circumspect man. He had to be, given his position, but it was his nature to be very measured in the things he said and not to give away too much. I used to wish I was more like Stefano. He didn't mind sharing his thoughts and never let the weight of the world settle on him. He knew how to laugh. And girls? Oh, they loved him."

"You do fine with the ladies," she pointed out.

"Ah, but the only lady that matters had a crush on him first." There was only rueful affection in his tone.

"You loved him very much."

"I loved all of them so much I didn't know how I would survive when I woke after the crash." His eyes grew wet. He didn't hide any of the agony he felt to this day. "I'd never felt so alone. So left behind."

"I'm sorry," she whispered, cupping the side of his face.

He held her hand there and said, "When I realized the crash had been deliberate... I had to do something, but righting one wrong wasn't enough. It became an obsession. A way to avoid addressing how empty my life was. Then, one day, there you were, a glimmer of gold in all the silt. But it was so complicated."

"I know," she murmured.

"When the possibility of a baby came up..." His eyes misted afresh. "I hadn't let myself love in a long time, but I felt the roots of it starting in me. I've never wanted anything more in my life than to have a family with you. You, Freja. I could see it so clearly, I could taste it. And then it was gone."

She swiped at a tickle on her cheek and her fingers came away wet. She leaned closer and he set his warm arm across her shoulders, nose to her temple.

"It locked me up again. It's really hard to say it. To admit that I love you and want your love. I'm terrified of how vulnerable I am to the pain of loss, but losing you, even to a damned airplane and a day of travel... I want you in my life, Freja. I need you."

"I want that, too," she admitted shakily. "I love you, too. So much. I'm sorry I left. I hated myself as soon as I did."

"Well, that will teach you." He gathered her into his lap. "Don't do it again."

Six months later...

"Everything looks perfectly normal except..."

They both lost their smiles. Giovanni's hand squeezed hers tighter. Freja swallowed.

"What's wrong?"

"Nothing. See for yourself." The technician pointed to the screen, then pointed to another spot on the screen, counting, "One, two. Twins."

"But..." Freja trailed off, speechless.

"This is very common with in vitro fertilizations..." The technician sent a glance to Giovanni's chair.

"But this was artificial insemination. I'm not using fertility drugs. They didn't implant embryos, just..."

"Ah." The technician looked closer. "There's only one placenta. Looks like you just got lucky."

They stayed lucky. Their identical twin

girls were born three weeks early at a clinic in Sicily, healthy and strong. They went home with their ecstatic parents a few days later.

EPILOGUE

HIS PASSPORT READ Benjamin Everhart. It was fake, but a good one. The border guard waved the small vanload of tourists along with only a cursory glance at it.

A few days of touring the sacred Paektu Mountain and Heaven Lake later, the van entered a small village. They were checked into a hotel approved for foreigners.

Everett double-checked he had the novel in his jacket pocket, then walked downstairs with a handful of airplane peanuts in his hand. The things he did for a friend.

He shoved the peanuts in his mouth and was gasping and losing consciousness before he'd reached his assigned table in the restaurant.

He woke in the clinic, an IV attached to his arm, throat still scratchy. An official stood by while a circumspect nurse checked his pulse. The woman disappeared and Everett motioned to the official that he wanted the book out of his jacket.

It was a British spy thriller. The official flipped through the pages, stopping to inspect the photo Everett was using for a bookmark. It was an image of Giovanni holding both his daughters. Louisa was trying to eat a button off his shirt. Teresa had one little fist tangled in Freja's hair as she crouched beside her husband's wheelchair. They were laughing at their girls' antics.

This was the tricky moment. Everett held his breath, wondering if the official would recognize her, but he only glanced at the blank backside, then stuffed the photo between the pages. He handed the book to Everett.

Everett set the photo on the side table and pretended to read.

Twenty minutes later, the doctor came in, gave him the North Korean brand of an antihistamine pen, and discharged him. Everett neglected to pick up the photo on his way out.

The next morning, as they were about to climb aboard the van, the same official pulled him aside.

Damn. That was never a good sign, but Everett kept an unbothered expression on his face.

A Korean woman offered him a small package and a silk scarf with cherry blossoms embroidered on it. The scarf was delicate and seemed valuable, but the woman motioned that this was to protect his still raw throat.

He got the message and put it on, bowing his thanks.

The official inspected the tea, sniffed it, and allowed him to board the bus.

When he gave Freja the scarf she cried into it, but for once Giovanni didn't scold him for interfering.

* * * * *

Captivated by
Confessions of an Italian Marriage?
*You won't be able to resist these
other stories by Dani Collins!*

Bound by Their Nine-Month Scandal
Cinderella's Royal Seduction
A Hidden Heir to Redeem Him
Beauty and Her One-Night Baby

Available now!